P9-DXJ-617

DATE DUE

FEB 07 8 2006 2018	NOV 7 2018		

Other Avon Books by
Beatrice Gormley

MAIL-ORDER WINGS

BEATRICE GORMLEY wrote and rewrote this story many times before it came out right. In fact, she says, "I wanted in the worst way for *my* fairy godmother to appear and write it for me!"

Mrs. Gormley lives in Duxbury, Massachusetts with her husband and two daughters.

EMILY ARNOLD McCULLY has illustrated many books and has recently written one of her own. She lives in Brooklyn, New York.

Fifth Grade Magic

Beatrice Gormley

Illustrated by Emily Arnold McCully

AN AVON CAMELOT BOOK

AVON BOOKS
A division of
The Hearst Corporation
1790 Broadway
New York, New York 10019

Copyright © 1982 by Beatrice Gormley
Text Illustrations Copyright © 1982 by Emily Arnold McCully
Editor: Ann Durrel
Designer: Isabel Warren-Lynch
Published by arrangement with E.P. Dutton, Inc.
Library of Congress Catalog Card Number: 82-9439
ISBN: 0-380-67439-4

The E.P. Dutton Inc. edition contains the following Library of
Congress Cataloging in Publication Data:

Gormley, Beatrice.   Fifth grade magic.

Summary: Devastated at not getting a part in the fifth
grade play, Gretchen is surprised when her desperation
conjures up a well-meaning but not very efficient
fairy godmother.
[1. Magic—Fiction.   2. School stories]
I. McCully, Emily Arnold, ill.   II. Title.
PZ7.G6696Fi   1982   [Fic]   82-9439

First Camelot Printing, February, 1984

CAMELOT TRADEMARK REG. U. S. PAT. OFF. AND IN
OTHER COUNTRIES, MARCA REGISTRADA, HECHO EN
U. S. A.

Printed in the U. S. A.

DON 10 9 8 7 6 5 4 3 2 1

to my husband, Bob
and
to my fairy godmother, Jane

Contents

1

The Rear View

Gretchen nudged Beth. "Look at Mrs. Sheppard," she whispered. "She looks like a hippopotamus."

Beth glanced up from her fractions work sheet. "Good grief," she muttered. "You mean a hippo*bottom*us."

Choking on a giggle, Gretchen gazed at the teacher, who was pinning papers on the bulletin board. Mrs. Sheppard liked to be in style, but this time she had picked the wrong style. She was wearing a gray skirtlike thing, really wide-legged knee-length pants. It made her seem—well, a lot larger than she was. "She must not have looked in the mirror this morning."

"I guess she didn't have a *rear*view mirror," said Beth. They had to cover their mouths to keep from laughing out loud.

Mrs. Sheppard looked over her shoulder, frowning at Gretchen and Beth's side of the classroom. "Let's keep our

1

eyes and our thoughts on our work, people." Then a push-pin dropped from her hand, and she bent over to pick it up.

As the teacher fumbled for the pushpin, looking even more like a hippobottomus, Gretchen heard someone whisper, "Ready—aim—fire!" It was Dennis Boyd, leaning out of his seat and aiming his pencil like a dart at Mrs. Sheppard.

Now the whole class was giggling. But Mrs. Sheppard, straightening to face them, didn't seem to have any idea what the joke was. She swept the class with a stern look. "We have some exciting news to talk about, but not until after your math work sheets are done. And no fairy godmother is going to wave her wand and solve the problems for you—you have to work them yourselves."

Mrs. Sheppard was always saying things like that. Gretchen wished a fairy godmother *would* appear, just to show the teacher up. Right in front of the chalkboard, waving her sparkly wand. *Bing!*—everyone's math problems solved.

Gretchen had already worked the last problem, anyway. While she waited for the others to finish their work sheets, she took a piece of scratch paper and began to doodle. Without thinking about it, she drew a person . . . the rear view . . . a woman wearing silly-looking skirt/pants. In fact, Gretchen realized, it was quite a good picture of Mrs. Sheppard, complete with upswept hairdo and with her head turned sideways to show her big glasses.

Putting down her pencil, Beth glanced over at what Gretchen was doing. Her eyes popped open wide, and a grin spread over her face. She mouthed silently, "That's really good, Gretchen!"

2

Gretchen thought so, too. She signed her name at the bottom of the picture, the way artists do. Then the girl on the other side of Beth poked her, wanting to see what was so interesting, and Beth slid the picture along the table to her. Gretchen heard a gasp and a smothered giggle.

"Everyone finished?" Mrs. Sheppard stood in front of the chalkboard, chalk in hand. "Very good—that's the kind of effort I like to see. Now for the fun. It's time to start working on the spring play!"

Gretchen sat up straight. At last! The fifth grade play. She had been waiting all year for this. And she was prepared. In the drama club, which Gretchen had started a few weeks ago, she and the other girls practiced acting at recess.

The teacher was writing the title of the play on the chalkboard: *Polly's Pies in Peril.* "We're going to put on an old-fashioned melodrama, people," she said. "In a melodrama, the audience can boo at the villain and cheer for the hero, which is such fun! Of course, we won't want to overdo it." Mrs. Sheppard smiled. Then she noticed Kathy, in the middle of the room, raising her hand. "Yes. What is it, Kathy?"

"I was just wondering, Mrs. Sheppard—are you going to direct the play this year?"

That was a good question, thought Gretchen. This was Mrs. Sheppard's first year of teaching fifth grade—she was really a second grade teacher. She might not know anything about directing plays. But Miss DiGrassi, the other fifth grade teacher, had been in charge of the play for years.

"Oh, no." Mrs. Sheppard spoke hastily. "Miss DiGrassi will direct the play. But I'm going to help her with the casting this afternoon, since she doesn't know most of you. And I want you to help me, people, by letting me know

3

what you would like to do to make this the best spring play ever." She paused to give Amy, the new girl sitting next to Kathy, an encouraging smile.

All right, thought Gretchen. Amy's been here since January—you don't have to baby her anymore.

"I'll list the characters and the backstage jobs on the board," Mrs. Sheppard went on, "and everyone who wants to work on the play, please write down your first, second, and third choices."

As the teacher began to write on the board, Gretchen saw a boy at the next table pass a piece of scratch paper to his neighbor, grinning and pointing at Mrs. Sheppard's back. It must be Gretchen's picture. She felt uneasy—she hadn't meant to let it get passed all over the class.

Now the other boy was holding the picture up, and Gretchen caught a glimpse of it. Oh, no. Something new had been added. Circles, one inside the other, like a dartboard target, drawn over the teacher's backside! Gretchen jumped up to grab the picture, but just then Mrs. Sheppard turned around. She sank back.

"You see, class, Winnie Winsum, the mother, has a little pie shop in her home. The heroine of the play is her beautiful daughter, Polly. . . ."

As Mrs. Sheppard talked, Gretchen forgot about the picture. The classroom seemed to fade away, and Gretchen saw herself on the stage at the end of the gym. The spotlight was on her, Polly Winsum, in her old-fashioned dress with a long, ruffled skirt. So beautiful, so good. In dreadful danger from the villainous Cadmun Blackheart.

A snicker from the middle of the room brought Gretchen out of her daydream. Her picture had traveled all the way over to Kathy! Gretchen made frantic motions to Kathy to hide the picture, but Kathy didn't seem to notice. She giggled out loud.

Mrs. Sheppard turned from the board again with a frown. Cutting off her giggle suddenly, Kathy slipped the piece of paper to Amy. But it was plain that Mrs. Sheppard had seen her do it. Gretchen felt her stomach sink.

"Kathy, I thought we all agreed at the beginning of the year that there was to be no note passing."

Kathy blinked innocently. "I wasn't passing notes, Mrs. Sheppard."

Gretchen wished with all her might that she could run time backwards, like film in a projector. Then the picture would pass from Amy to Kathy, to the boys at the next table, to the girl on the other side of Beth, to Beth, and at last back to Gretchen, who would un-draw her hippobottomus portrait of Mrs. Sheppard.

But time did not roll magically backwards. The picture was still in front of Amy, who was gaping as if it were a hand grenade. Nervously she twisted a lock of her long blonde hair.

With a jab Mrs. Sheppard pushed her pink-lensed glasses up on her nose. "Amy, please bring that paper to me." She added more gently, "Of course I'm not blaming *you*."

Now Gretchen was going to get it. Why had she let them pass the picture around? Why, oh, *why* had she signed her name?

Mrs. Sheppard took the picture from Amy and stared at it, pressing her lips together tightly. Her eyes rested for an instant at the bottom of the picture, narrowing. Then she crumpled the paper and dropped it in the wastebasket. Not

6

even looking in Gretchen's direction, the teacher glanced at the clock. "Time to line up for lunch. It's outside recess today, people, so take your sweaters and jackets."

It was the best kind of day you could expect in March—cold, but bright and not too windy. At recess, Gretchen and Beth and Kathy and the other girls in the drama club gathered near the edge of the woods that bordered the playing field. Here the ground rose a few feet into a flat-topped knoll, useful for a stage.

"Kathy, thanks a lot for getting me into trouble," said Gretchen.

"Yeah," said Beth. "That wasn't too bright."

"Me—?" Kathy sputtered. "*I* didn't draw that picture of Mrs. Sheppard. *I* didn't pass it around. Anyway," she went on in a reasonable tone, "you didn't get into any trouble. Mrs. Sheppard didn't do anything."

"She didn't do anything *yet*, " said Beth. "She might be thinking up some fate worse than death."

"Oh, well," said Gretchen. She was still irritated with Kathy, but she didn't want to spend the recess arguing. She looked around at the others. "Let's start the scene. Hey, wasn't it a good thing we've been practicing acting? I knew the play was coming up soon." She took a paperback book from the pocket of her jacket. "This time Beth can be the spy, and—"

"Just a minute." Kathy motioned toward another group of girls, playing foursquare on the paved space near the building. "Why don't we ask Amy if she wants to be in the drama club? She'd be good."

Gretchen raised her eyebrows. "Amy Sacher? What makes you think—"

7

But the other girls were murmuring. "Yeah, let's ask Amy." "It would be nice—she's new." "I wish I had long blonde hair like hers." "She's going to be a model, you know."

"Good grief," said Beth to Gretchen. But Kathy was already trotting across the field, dodging the boys playing soccer. She waved at Amy, standing in the foursquare line.

Gretchen tried again. "Let's get started, anyway." But the others paid no attention. They were squinting into the bright sunlight, watching Kathy talk to Amy.

From this distance the most noticeable thing about the two girls was their long hair, Kathy's dark and Amy's blonde. Strands of it blew across their faces as they talked. Gretchen saw that they were both wearing their hair pulled back with big barrettes. Was Amy copying Kathy, or the other way around?

After a moment's conversation, Amy shook her head. Kathy said something, shrugged, and trotted back toward the drama club.

The group waited expectantly as Kathy ran up, panting. "Amy said she'd rather play foursquare."

"Fine," said Gretchen, jumping up on the rise. "Let's stop wasting time. If Beth's the spy, then—"

"I'm sort of tired of acting myself," said Kathy loudly. "I don't see why we have to practice anymore when we're going to be doing the play in school." She stared at Gretchen. "I think I'll start a new foursquare game."

"Me too," said one of the girls.

"Hey, yeah, let's all play foursquare!" Another girl stopped and glanced apologetically at Gretchen. "It's getting kind of boring, just acting every day."

8

Boring! Gretchen couldn't believe what she was hearing. "You can't be good actors without practicing."

But they were all drifting after Kathy, who was halfway across the playground again.

Gretchen watched them go, her teeth clenched. Then she looked down from the rise at Beth, the only remaining member of the drama club. "Don't you want to play four-square?" she asked bitterly.

"It might be fun for a change," said Beth in a soothing tone. But she made no move to go.

Gretchen kicked at the winter-brown grass, making heel marks in the damp ground. "They're so stupid. I don't know why they think Amy's so great, with her sweetie-sweet smile. And they don't even care that much about the spring play!" Her voice rose in disbelief. "I've been think-ing about being in the play ever since I was in kindergar-ten!"

"Really?" Beth sounded sympathetic but surprised. "I don't even remember what play they put on when we were in kindergarten."

"It was *Cinderella,*" said Gretchen. "Kathy's older sister was the fairy godmother, and the star fell off her wand. Don't you remember that?"

"Oh, yeah." Beth giggled. "Anyway, the play for this year sounds pretty good. *Polly's Pies in Peril.* What part did you ask for?"

"Polly Winsum," said Gretchen without hesitating. Then she glanced sharply at Beth. Gretchen wanted very badly to play the heroine, but she would hate it if she beat out Beth for the part. "You didn't—what part did you ask for?"

"Spotlight technician," said Beth.

9

Gretchen's jaw dropped. "But—but that isn't even a part! Don't you want to be in the play? I bet you could get the part of the mother, or the neighbor, at least."

Beth shrugged. "I think I'd rather work the spotlight. I got tired of learning lines in the drama club. Anyway"—she grinned—"if I'm working the spotlight, I'll shine it on you all the time."

A warm feeling of friendship came over Gretchen. Beth wasn't any more serious about acting than the other girls, but she had stuck by Gretchen anyway. "Okay, sounds good to me." Gretchen stepped down from the rise. "We can't act out a scene with only two people. I guess we might as well go play foursquare."

2

A Celebrity in Our Midst

In school the next morning, the girls' coat closet smelled like vinyl slickers and damp wool. Wrinkling her nose, Gretchen tugged off her boots, added them to the line inside the closet, and padded to her table to put her shoes on. "Hi, Beth."

"Hi." Beth was twirling one of her brown braids, staring at the windows across the room. "Yuck. Inside recess."

Glancing up from her shoelaces, Gretchen saw the sleet sliding down the panes, blurring the dark, bare trees and dingy grass outside. "Oh, well," she said cheerfully. She took her pencil box out of her book bag, removed her special pencil with the fluffy end, and placed it on the table, ready to write. "At least we'll find out who gets which part in the play." She looked up at the chalkboard, where the characters and the backstage jobs were still listed. Polly Winsum, heroine.

"I wonder how Mrs. Sheppard will pick kids for the parts,

though," said Beth thoughtfully. "She's never seen any of us act."

"No, but she could tell who would be a good actor from other things—like who reads with expression, who has a good loud voice, who doesn't mind getting up in front of the class. Things like that." Gretchen spoke confidently. She did all those things well.

By now the other children had taken their places at Gretchen and Beth's table, and the classroom was almost full. As the teacher opened her attendance book, Gretchen studied her face. Mrs. Sheppard *did* understand how to pick actors, didn't she? She would have to see that Gretchen should have a big part, anyway. But Gretchen didn't want just any big part—she wanted to play Polly Winsum, heroine.

A hand with small, slim fingers reached in front of Gretchen, stroking the fluffy end of her pencil. It was Amy. "That's cute, Gretchen," she said. "Your pencil looks like a weird little person, with those googly eyes."

Picking up her pencil, Gretchen smoothed the tuft of orange fluff on the eraser end. "Thanks," she said coolly. Amy might charm everyone else, but she wasn't going to charm Gretchen. Not after breaking up the drama club.

Amy hesitated, as if she wanted to say something else, but now Mrs. Sheppard was raising her hand for silence. Amy hurried to her seat in the middle of the room.

Picking up a newspaper clipping from her desk, Mrs. Sheppard waved it in front of the class. "People, does everyone know we have a celebrity in our midst?" Beaming at Amy, she pushed her glasses up on her nose with one finger. "This article was in last night's paper—'Modeling Career Launched.'"

As Mrs. Sheppard began to read the article out loud, everyone turned to look at Amy. Next to Amy, Kathy was almost jumping out of her seat with excitement. But Amy gazed down at the table, her eyelashes shadowing her cheeks.

Pretending to be modest, thought Gretchen. How sweet. Watching Mrs. Sheppard reading, she wondered, as she had wondered before, why anyone would wear glasses with pink lenses. They might be in style, but they made Mrs. Sheppard's eyes look red and tired. "I see the world through rose-colored glasses," Mrs. Sheppard had joked on the first day of school. Ha-ha, thought Gretchen. She certainly sees Amy through rose-colored glasses.

Pinning the article next to a picture of pussy willows on the bulletin board, Mrs. Sheppard picked up a stack of dictionaries. "Paper monitor—that's you today, Kathy— pass out lined paper." She moved among the tables, giving out the dictionaries. "Everyone copy the vocabulary words from your reader and look up each definition. Remember, people, practice your handwriting every time you write."

The morning dragged on. Each time Mrs. Sheppard opened her mouth to speak to the class, Gretchen was sure she was going to announce the parts for the play. Her heart would start to race. But then Mrs. Sheppard would only call up another reading group.

Could Mrs. Sheppard have forgotten? Gretchen looked up from her paper of Did You Understand? reading questions. The teacher was walking up to the chalkboard. Gretchen decided to ask her about the play. "Mrs. Sheppard?"

But at the same moment, the teacher said, "People, pencils down, all eyes on me. Please don't interrupt,

Gretchen." She looked around the classroom, chalk poised, until the murmuring died down. "Miss DiGrassi and I got together yesterday after school and assigned responsibilities for *Polly's Pies in Peril.*" She pointed to the name of the play at the top of the board. "Now, before I announce the parts and other jobs, I want to make it clear that there is no *un-*important work to be done on the play. Every part, every job is important! If the spotlight technician"—Beth sat up straight—"doesn't turn on the spotlight, the audience won't see the heroine. If the townsperson who has only two lines doesn't say them correctly, the villain won't get his cue." Mrs. Sheppard smiled brightly around the room. "Plays don't happen by magic. We'll all have to work our hardest."

Gretchen twiddled her fluffy-ended pencil. Yes, we know, Mrs. Sheppard. Plays don't happen by magic. Just announce the parts!

But now, finally, the teacher was writing names next to the list of characters and backstage jobs. "Winnie Winsum, the mother, is Jennifer Bell, from Miss DiGrassi's class. The Winsums' neighbor will be Kathy. Spotlight technician—Beth McEvoy."

Beth turned to Gretchen, mouth open in delight. She bounced in her seat.

Gretchen smiled and shrugged. If that's what made Beth happy—

"Polly Winsum—Amy Sacher."

Mrs. Sheppard's words punched Gretchen in the stomach, making her gasp. She stared disbelievingly at the teacher, who was beaming over her shoulder at Amy as she wrote.

Amy turned to Kathy with a big smile, clapping silently.

Now Mrs. Sheppard was writing on the other side of the board. "Scenery manager—Gretchen Nichols. This work will make use of Gretchen's artistic ability." Somebody in the back snickered, but Mrs. Sheppard didn't look at Gretchen or smile.

Mrs. Sheppard hates me, thought Gretchen.

She felt as if the teacher had slapped her in the face. A teacher couldn't make decisions, like who got which parts in a play, according to likes and dislikes.

But that's just what Mrs. Sheppard was doing.

It was one thing for Gretchen, who was a kid, to pass a funny picture of Mrs. Sheppard around the class. It was another thing for Mrs. Sheppard, the grown-up teacher, to shut Gretchen out of the play.

How could she?

The teacher went on writing and talking, but the buzz of comments and laughter seemed far away from Gretchen, as if she were in a glass booth. Polly Winsum—Amy Sacher. Scenery manager—Gretchen Nichols. She felt a trembling inside, as if she might scream right out in class, "It's not fair!" To keep the scream down, she squeezed her hands together hard, clasping her wispy-headed pencil between them.

"Cadmun Blackheart," Mrs. Sheppard was saying. "The banker—and what else is he, people?"

"The villain," said several boys and girls.

"Right! Cadmun Blackheart—Dennis Boyd."

Gretchen glanced up. Dennis pretended to fall off his chair in horror. There were whistles and cheers around the classroom, and the boy sitting next to Dennis punched his shoulder. "Oh, Dennis is a bad, bad man!"

Shaking his blond forelock out of his eyes, Dennis called out, "I said I wanted to be a stagehand!"

Calmly Mrs. Sheppard said, "I think you'll find you can really get into this part, Dennis." Gretchen noticed the teacher didn't look at him, either. "Where was I? Oh—townspeople."

"Dennis Boyd, the villain," whispered Beth to Gretchen. "Typecasting!"

Gretchen couldn't even smile. She stared down at her pencil, smoothing the fluffy orange hair straight up. The pupils of the plastic eyes wobbled, astonished.

Gretchen heard chalk squeaking on the board and Mrs. Sheppard's voice going up and down, but she couldn't bear to look at the board or listen to what the teacher was saying. She wished she never had to hear Mrs. Sheppard's voice again. It's not fair, she said silently to her pencil. I've been waiting for five years. I've even been practicing acting to get ready for the play!

The pencil nodded sympathetically.

Amy just moved to town this winter! And she didn't even want to join the drama club. And she gets her picture in the paper, and everyone's so impressed with her. Why should she get the part?

The pencil didn't know. It shook its head, baffled.

"Gretchen."

Feeling a nudge from Beth, Gretchen looked up. Mrs. Sheppard had said her name.

"—understudy," the teacher was saying. "So you have two important duties instead of just one." She put her chalk down. "Time to line up for lunch, people. Leave your coats in the closets—inside recess today."

"No kidding," said Beth softly to Gretchen. She nodded at the sleet still streaking the windows.

Gretchen stood up, frowning at the board. "What did Mrs. Sheppard say about understudies?"

"She said you were the understudy for Polly Winsum. I'm the understudy for the mother."

Gretchen looked away from the sympathy in Beth's eyes. She would *not* cry in front of everybody, especially the teacher.

Turning from Beth, Gretchen joined the line forming at the door. To avoid meeting anyone's eyes, she stared at the bulletin board beside her. Pussy willows. Papers with red-penciled A's at the top. And a newspaper clipping: "Modeling Career Launched."

Gretchen's stomach tightened. She didn't want to look at the newspaper picture, but she couldn't pull her eyes away from it. It showed Amy, her long blonde hair flowing over her shoulders, sitting in front of a backdrop, smiling at a photographer. A lean, stylish-looking woman—she must be Amy's mother—watched them with a pleased expression.

Amy's modeling career was launched. Gretchen's acting career was sunk.

Later that afternoon Gretchen plodded past the spruce trees beside her driveway. The sleet had turned into drizzle, but it had been a long, cold, wet walk, and her book bag dragged at her arm. At least now she could make herself a cup of cocoa and tell her mother what had happened. Gretchen pulled open the back door. "Mom?"

But even before she pushed back the hood of her slicker, Gretchen knew this was not the afternoon to look for sympathy. From the living room the vacuum cleaner whined urgently, and the kitchen reeked of some kind of sauce with wine in it—ugh. Mom wouldn't be cooking and cleaning like this unless they were having company for dinner tonight. Well, that might not be so bad. Maybe it was Gretchen's Aunt Marianne and her boyfriend Paul.

Unsnapping her slicker, Gretchen clumped through the laundry room and into the kitchen. "Mom?"

"Gretchen?" The noise of the vacuum cut off with a snarl, and her mother, wild-haired, appeared in the doorway to the dining room. Gretchen's baby brother Jason crawled up behind Mrs. Nichols and pulled himself upright, holding on to her leg. "Hi. I need your help, because —Gretchen! You go right back into the laundry room with those boots! Here I am running around like a crazy person, trying to get the house cleaned up and fix something impressive for dinner and watch Jason, and you track in mud!"

A nice welcome, thought Gretchen, but she retreated to the laundry room. "Who's coming—Marianne?" she called as she pulled her boots off.

"I wish it were," said her mother. "I wouldn't have to knock myself out for Marianne and Paul. It's some business people Daddy invited to dinner tonight. And I couldn't leave my office as soon as I hoped to, because I had a new client and had to go over his accounts with him and explain that I couldn't magically solve *all* his problems for him. And this place is such a horrible MESS!" As Gretchen stepped back into the kitchen, she went on, "Now *please* do not put your books down here. Take them right up to your room, and I mean your room, not just putting them on the stairs to take up later. And also take that sweater that's been

19

hanging on the back of the rocker for six days." Mrs. Nichols pointed across the kitchen.

How could her mother talk to her like this? Not even "How was your day at school?" let alone "Did you get the part you wanted in the play?"

And her sweater *hadn't* been there for six days. "I only left it there yesterday," muttered Gretchen, snatching the sweater from the back of the rocker. She stuffed it into her book bag and charged at the stairs, swinging her leg over the baby gate.

"And after you put your things away, please come back downstairs and help tidy up," called her mother. The giant-mosquito hum of the vacuum started up again.

As Gretchen reached the top of the stairs, she heard Jason begin to howl over the vacuum cleaner noise. Gretchen felt like howling herself. Mom would put Jason in the playpen and give him a teething biscuit, and he would be fine, but what about her?

Gretchen dropped her book bag on the floor of her room. Yes, what about Gretchen? What could she do? How could she stand it?

And especially, how could Mrs. Sheppard treat her like that? Gretchen had known, even before the teacher saw her drawing, that she wasn't Mrs. Sheppard's favorite pupil. But she never dreamed the teacher might do something that would hurt the play.

Now Gretchen began to see how the teacher might have been thinking. Mrs. Sheppard didn't know anything about plays or about who would be the best actor. All she knew was that she could do something nice for Amy by making her the heroine and punish Gretchen by not giving her any part in the play at all.

It was Gretchen, not Mrs. Sheppard, who had made the big mistake. If Gretchen had understood the teacher, she never would have drawn her rear view. . . . Well, anyway, she wouldn't have let it be passed around the class. She would have been polite and sweet to Mrs. Sheppard, starting in September. Oh, why hadn't she been?

But maybe it wouldn't have made any difference. Maybe Mrs. Sheppard would have chosen Amy anyway, because Amy was prettier.

That idea gave Gretchen an odd, helpless feeling. Stepping in front of the mirror over the dresser, she leaned forward to look into her own blue gray eyes. Her ginger-colored hair, damp from walking home through the rain, curled over her forehead and around her ears.

No, she didn't look like the kind of girl who could be a model. She looked pretty ordinary. But I'm not ordinary! thought Gretchen. I'm—me!

She had to get someone to help her, maybe someone who could reason with Mrs. Sheppard.

But who?

"No fairy godmother is going to wave her wand and solve the problem for you," Mrs. Sheppard's voice seemed to say coldly in Gretchen's head.

"Yes, she is!" burst out Gretchen furiously. "Fairy godmother, come on! It's me, Gretchen! Help!" And then she was surprised to find herself sobbing aloud.

She remembered how Mrs. Sheppard had looked right past her, as if she didn't exist. She remembered all the heads in the class turning toward Amy, as if she were a star already. Sitting down on her desk chair, Gretchen put her face in her hands and cried.

After a minute or two, in spite of feeling so awful,

21

Gretchen wondered how she would look, crying like this. She raised her head to check the mirror.

She couldn't see the mirror!

Abruptly Gretchen stopped crying and sat up. She couldn't see the mirror because there was something in front of it. A fuzzy image, like an out-of-focus picture from a movie projector, had appeared in the middle of Gretchen's room. It looked more solid than a movie, although Gretchen could see the outline of her dresser behind it.

"Errora to the rescue!" shouted a high, faraway voice.

Gretchen wiped tears from her cheeks with the back of her hand. Blinking, she watched the picture grow sharper. It was a small, round-faced woman, no taller than Gretchen. Her baggy, drab blue skirt flapped around her ankles, and her baggy, drab blue jacket was rolled up at the sleeves. Her hair was pulled back in a bun and topped with a blue visored cap, and she carried something that looked like a calculator.

Smiling as if she were very pleased with herself, the woman said, "Agent Errora, designated representative to Sector 87. It is hoped that service can be rendered."

3

Errora to the Rescue

Gretchen stared. At first she thought that somehow, without a set, she must be seeing a TV picture. She knew it was possible to hear a radio station without a radio if you had braces on your teeth.

But Gretchen didn't have braces.

This little woman was dressed sort of like a postman. Did the post office have a special TV sender?

The woman cleared her throat. "This is Sector 87, isn't it? Aren't you the girl Gretchen?" There was a note of anxiety in her voice.

"How—how did you know my name?" Gretchen felt silly, talking to a TV picture.

"How?" The woman looked surprised. "You identified yourself in your call." She pushed a button on her calculatorlike thing.

Gretchen heard a scratchy voice—could that be *her*

voice? "Fairy godmother, come on! It's me, Gretchen!"

"And I, Errora, was on duty—so here I am." The little woman smiled uncertainly.

So this person (Errora?) had somehow overheard Gretchen. Maybe she had seen her crying, too. Gretchen felt her face burn. "It was none of your business."

"None of my—!" Errora looked crushed. Her lower lip began to tremble. "You don't want me to render assistance after all?"

Gretchen was afraid Errora might start crying, too. "I didn't mean that," she said hastily. "But—"

"Well, then." Errora gave a happy sigh. "Here I am, ready to assess your situational obstacles and fix everything up just dandy—I mean, apply measures of a corrective nature, utilizing the resources of my Enchantulator." She waved the calculatorlike object.

"That's very nice of you," said Gretchen. She hesitated. Could Errora have escaped from a mental hospital? Maybe that's why her uniform was too big for her—maybe it was really a guard's uniform. Gretchen noticed the insignia sewn on Errora's sleeve and on the front of her cap: a sparkling wand. She had gone to a lot of trouble to make Gretchen think she was her fairy godmother.

Anyway, it wouldn't hurt to tell her what Gretchen's problem was. "I don't think anyone can do anything for me, though. Mrs. Sheppard loves Amy and hates me, and she's already picked Amy for the best part in the play."

"Yes? Please continue." Errora spoke in an important tone. "I must become aware of all the relevant factors before I can assess your situational obstacles."

"Well . . ." Gretchen didn't know what good it would do,

24

but at least someone wanted to listen to her. "You see, every year the fifth grade in my school puts on a play. And there's a new girl in my class, Amy, with long blonde hair. Everyone thinks she's so wonderful. . . ." As Gretchen told her story, she began to tremble again, felt like screaming again. ". . . and I've been waiting for the play ever since I was in kindergarten! It's not fair!" Her last words came out with a squeak.

Errora had been listening intently, fiddling with the keys on the thing she called her Enchantulator. Now she announced, "Problem: rival with long blonde hair. Solution —just a minute." She punched one more key and peered at the display window. "Solution: abbreviatize." She smiled triumphantly at Gretchen.

"Do what?" asked Gretchen blankly.

"Yes! Cut Amy's hair. Then her power will be broken, and your teacher will reassign her part in the play to you."

Errora was crazy, no doubt about it.

Still, Gretchen liked the idea of scissors shearing off Amy's long blonde hair. "But she'd never let me do it."

Errora smiled patiently. "You don't have to do anything. Your problems are currently assigned to me and will be solved with the programmatic resources of my Enchantulator. All I need is a pictorial representation of your rival."

"A picture of Amy? But I don't—" Gretchen paused, remembering the newspaper picture of Amy. It would probably be in this morning's paper, on the floor beside the rocker in the kitchen.

It couldn't hurt to let Errora try.

"Hold on." Gretchen dashed out of her bedroom.

Her mother, feeding Jason in his high chair, gave her a

25

grateful look as Gretchen picked up the newspaper. "Thanks, darling. I'm glad I didn't have to ask you to do that."

Gretchen smiled sweetly and carried the paper to the garage, pausing to tear out Amy's picture. Then she ran back through the kitchen and up to her bedroom again.

"Very good," said Errora, looking closely at the picture. "Just hold it up at arm's length in a stable manner"—she held up her own baggy-sleeved arm—"and relax while I chant."

Breathless, Gretchen sat down on her bed and watched Errora thrust the Enchantulator out toward Amy's picture. A beam of light shone from the edge of the instrument, playing back and forth across Amy's waist-length hair. Errora chanted,

Although heretofore exhibiting hair of a lengthy nature,
She will be compelled to accept a certain curtailment.
And furthermore,
She will experience a diminished function of influence.

What is she saying? wondered Gretchen. It sounded like English, but she couldn't understand half the words.

The beam of light flicked out. "Finalized," said Errora in a satisfied voice. "No, don't thank me now. I'll come back tomorrow at the same time for a debriefing."

"Wait." Gretchen had a lot of questions to ask Errora, beginning with how she got into Gretchen's room. Besides — "I can't come right home from school! I have ballet class tomorrow afternoon."

But Errora was gone, as if someone had switched off a projector.

Or—as if Gretchen had just awakened from a dream.

4

The Fateful Haircut

"Amy cut her hair!" Beth dropped into her chair beside Gretchen, staring across the room.

"I know," said Gretchen, trying not to gape at Amy's cropped head. A thrill of excitement mixed with fright shortened her breath. Errora wasn't a dream. And she wasn't a crazy lady on TV, either. She had really worked magic with that thing she called an Enchantulator.

And what a thorough job Errora had done! Gretchen had imagined Amy's hair cut to the middle of her neck, a little shorter than Gretchen's. But Errora had chopped it off over her ears, well above the white collar of her plaid blouse.

Gretchen felt a twinge of guilt. How could Amy stand to come to school with her beautiful long hair gone?

The odd thing was that Amy didn't look upset—she was calmly taking out her pencils and pencil sharpener. Trying to act as if nothing had happened, was she? Gretchen almost felt sorry for her.

But had Amy worried about Gretchen's feelings when Mrs. Sheppard assigned the parts for the play? No, she hadn't. So, too bad for her.

Now Kathy was coming into the room, unslinging her backpack from her shoulders—and stopping stock-still. "Amy!" Kathy let her backpack plop down on Amy's table. "You got your hair cut."

Gretchen strained her ears. What would Amy answer?

Amy looked up from her pencil sharpener, smiling. "Hi. Isn't it a nice cut? Mr. Jobbins did it. He's my mother's hairdresser." She shook her head. "See how it falls back into place when I do that? And I won't have any more snarls!" She made a face. "I hated combing my hair when it was long."

Gretchen could hardly believe her ears. Amy had cut her hair on purpose? Had Errora cast a spell on her mind, too, to make her think that?

For a moment Kathy just stood looking at Amy. She opened her mouth and shut it without saying anything. Then, pulling a strand of her own dark hair over her shoulder, she nodded. "Yeah, I hate snarls, too." She slid into her chair, gazing at Amy with her head on one side. "That really is a nice cut. A lot of famous ice skaters wear their hair like that."

What was going on? Gretchen, her eyes fixed on Amy's hair, seemed to see it change from hacked-off long hair to a shining golden cap, cut skillfully to the shape of Amy's head.

Now Gretchen didn't know what to think. In a way she was glad Amy wasn't upset. If Amy liked her haircut, then Gretchen hadn't done anything wrong. Maybe she had even done Amy a favor.

29

But that wasn't the idea!

On the other hand—it didn't matter whether Amy liked her haircut or not, as long as Mrs. Sheppard gave Gretchen her part in the play. *That* was the important thing about Errora's spell.

The table between Amy's and Gretchen's was full now, so that Gretchen couldn't see Amy very well. Three or four girls clustered around Amy, chattering and smiling. A boy yelled, "Wow! Amy got her hair cut. Hey, Dennis, she looks just like you!"

Gretchen's startled glance shot across the room to Dennis Boyd. Amy, look like *Dennis*? His blond forelock fell across his eyes as he wrestled with one of the boys at his table. His plaid flannel shirttail hung outside his pants.

"Good morning, people." Mrs. Sheppard's heels clicked as she hurried into the room.

In an instant Dennis was in his seat with his hands folded, an angelic expression on his face. What do you know, thought Gretchen. Now he does look sort of like Amy.

Mrs. Sheppard slipped her coat off and picked up the attendance book. "And what a beautiful morning! My crocuses are blooming. Are anyone else's—why, Amy!" Letting the attendance book fall to her desk, the teacher leaned forward on her fingertips. "Your hair."

Amy smiled at Mrs. Sheppard, touching the back of her neck. "I got it cut. My mother thought it would be a good idea."

"Your mother—" Mrs. Sheppard looked puzzled, almost angry. "But— Couldn't you have waited until after the play? Your long hair was just right for an old-fashioned heroine."

30

I knew it! thought Gretchen. That's why Mrs. Sheppard picked Amy for Polly Winsum—because of her hair.

"Gee, I'm sorry, Mrs. Sheppard," said Amy. "I guess Mother didn't think of that."

Mrs. Sheppard looked as if she wanted to say something more, but then she shut her mouth and marched to the closet to hang up her coat.

Watching her, Gretchen felt hope rising in her chest. Mrs. Sheppard seemed really annoyed. Hadn't Errora said that cutting Amy's hair would break her power over the teacher? And that the teacher would take the heroine's part away from Amy and give it to Gretchen? Maybe this afternoon, when they read the play . . .

Today was class picture day. Before lunch, Mrs. Sheppard lined the class up by twos and marched them down the stairs toward the gym, where the photographer was taking the pictures. Dennis and another boy were behind Gretchen and Beth in line. Glancing back at Dennis, Beth pulled her braids forward and held them under her chin, out of harm's way.

"Sh!" said Mrs. Sheppard as twenty-six pairs of feet clattered on the stairs. "Other classes are trying to work." She darted up and down the line. "Quiet feet and mouths, people! Other classes are trying to work."

"They can't hear themselves think anyway, with all the racket you're making." Dennis's voice wasn't quite loud enough for the teacher to hear, but his remark set off giggles up and down the line. Mrs. Sheppard hurried up the stairs.

"Sh!" She bent toward them, frowning. "Other classes are trying to work."

31

When the teacher had gone back to the front of the line, Gretchen turned to grin at Dennis. She liked him, even if he was a wise guy and a nuisance.

In the gym the photographer spent several minutes arranging the children in three rows. The first row sat on folding chairs, the second row stood behind them on the floor, and the third row stood on chairs behind the second row. Gretchen and Beth were ordered to the end of the third row. "And the blond twins in the middle," said the photographer.

Blond twins? Gretchen stretched her neck to see where he was pointing. There weren't any twins in Mrs. Sheppard's class. But then she caught sight of the backs of two cropped blond heads.

"He means Amy and Dennis." Beth giggled. "He thinks they're twins!" The gym echoed with laughter and comments.

"All right, you aren't twins," said the photographer impatiently. "Just stand together in the middle row." He squinted through his camera.

"No way!" shouted Dennis, jumping into the back row. The metal chairs clanged.

"Dennis!" said Mrs. Sheppard. "Please don't hold us up."

"Never mind," said the photographer. "It was just an idea. All right, young lady, the blonde girl, you stand in the middle by yourself."

Obediently Amy wiggled through the other children to her place behind the first row of chairs.

"What a close call!" Dennis muttered. "I was almost a twin."

Later that afternoon, Mrs. Sheppard passed out the scripts for the play. "Miss DiGrassi asked me to have you read it through once before she starts working with you. Those of you who are *not* actors or understudies may go to the library for free reading time—quietly!"

Gretchen took a script, sitting up straighter. Surely now Errora's magic would work, and Mrs. Sheppard would give Gretchen the part of Polly Winsum. When Amy started reading, it would dawn on Mrs. Sheppard that she was all wrong for the part.

First the teacher had them write their names on the script and mark their own lines with a bright crayon. Underlining Polly Winsum's lines in yellow, Gretchen felt a glow of satisfaction. Polly had more lines than any of the other characters—it was clear she was the star.

Then they started reading the play. Beth read Winnie Winsum's lines, since the girl playing the mother was in Miss DiGrassi's class. Gretchen sat silently, watching Mrs. Sheppard each time Amy spoke for Polly Winsum. Amy read without stumbling, but there wasn't any expression in her voice. She might as well have been reading a math problem. Surely Mrs. Sheppard would notice that. Maybe she would ask Gretchen to read Polly Winsum's part for a while—then she would see how much better Gretchen could play the part.

The script reading dragged on to Cadmun Blackheart's first entrance. "How fortunate that Mama and I are able to earn a modest income from the tasty pies we bake," read Amy. "Otherwise, we could never pay Mr. Blackheart, the banker, the mortgage installments on our humble but cozy home."

33

Gretchen's attention had wandered. She was wondering again whether she had imagined Errora after all. Or maybe Errora was real, but she was a post office clerk gone crazy. Maybe it was just coincidence that Amy's mother had decided to take her to get her hair cut yesterday afternoon.

"Someone's not paying attention," said Mrs. Sheppard sharply.

Gretchen's head jerked up, but the teacher was frowning across the room at Dennis. He was entertaining his friends by poking his nose and sticking out his tongue, as if his nose were a button that operated his tongue.

"That's your cue, Cadmun Blackheart."

Dennis looked blankly up at the teacher, then down at the script. He began flipping pages.

He doesn't even want to be in the play, thought Gretchen. Why did Mrs. Sheppard give him the part? Maybe to punish him.

With help from the boy next to him, Dennis found his place. "Aha, my pretty," he mumbled.

"Try to speak up, Dennis," said Mrs. Sheppard. "When we put on the play, we want everyone in the back of the gym to hear us."

"Aha!" bellowed Dennis.

"Your normal voice will do." Her own voice tight with control, Mrs. Sheppard folded her arms.

The reading droned on and on. Letting her thoughts drift, Gretchen suddenly found her eyes focused on the clock. It was 2:45, almost the end of the school day. If Mrs. Sheppard was going to take Amy's part away and give it to Gretchen, she would have to do it pretty quick.

" 'I am so distressed,' " Amy was reading calmly. " 'We have not sold one pie all week. Boo, hoo, hoo.' "

34

Gretchen's eyes were glued to Mrs. Sheppard. Her heart raced. The teacher had to see it now. Distressed! Amy didn't even sound mildly worried. Her bad acting, together with the haircut, would make up the teacher's mind.

Mrs. Sheppard glanced up from her copy of the script. "What a nice, distinct voice, Amy! People, I want every one of you to speak as loudly and clearly as that for Miss Di-Grassi." Pushing her glasses up on her nose, the teacher looked at the clock. "We won't have time to finish reading the play after all. But everyone take your scripts home and practice reading them aloud. You'll start meeting with Miss DiGrassi tomorrow afternoon."

The door of the classroom swung open—the boys and girls who had gone to the library were coming back. Gretchen's heart sank lower and lower. So that was that.

Amy would play Polly Winsum, even without her long blonde hair, whether she said her lines like a robot or not.

Gretchen looked out the window at the sunshine on the brownish lawn, at the branches stretching toward the blue sky. It all seemed gray to her. There had been no magic working in this day after all.

Blinking back angry tears, Gretchen went to the coat closet to get her jacket. If she ever saw—or imagined she saw—Errora again, she would give her a piece of her mind.

5

No Sympathy

Gretchen's mother picked her up from school, as she always did on ballet class days. After ballet Mrs. Nichols made stops at the post office, the drugstore, and the A&P, while Gretchen stayed beside Jason's car seat and let him play with the zipper pull on her jacket. She also found a pussy willow catkin in her jacket pocket and tickled his chin with it.

"I appreciate your keeping him amused, darling." Gretchen's mother was stowing groceries in the back of the station wagon. "He's so fussy this afternoon—he must be teething."

By the time they turned in their driveway, the setting sun was glowing red in the clear sky behind the spruces. "Quarter to six!" said Mrs. Nichols, balancing Jason on her hip to open the back door. "It was so sunny and light this afternoon, I didn't realize how late it was getting."

Late? Gretchen frowned as she hung up her jacket. Was

36

she late for something? Oh. Errora had said she would reappear in Gretchen's room this afternoon. Of course, if Gretchen had just imagined Errora, everything Errora said was imaginary, too.

Her mother set Jason down on the kitchen floor, but he began to whimper, the kind of whimper that tended to change into a howl. "Oh, dear. Gretchen, would you feed Jason some cheese while I start dinner?" Taking cheese from the refrigerator, Mrs. Nichols cut it into cubes. "He must be starved—he didn't have any snack this afternoon." She unclamped the tray from Jason's high chair and hoisted him into it.

Gretchen hadn't minded entertaining Jason in the car, but now something was urging her to run up to her room and check, just in case. "Okay—I'll be right back." She edged toward the stairs.

"Gretchen!" Her mother looked exasperated. "Please, look after Jason so I can fix dinner. I'm starved myself, aren't you?"

"But—" Gretchen bit her lip. She couldn't very well say, "But my fairy godmother might be waiting for me upstairs." Her mother was now peeling an onion over the sink, head bent, as if the matter were settled. Gretchen couldn't think of an urgent-sounding excuse for going to her room. And she *was* hungry.

Taking the saucer of cheese cubes from the counter, Gretchen popped a cube into her own mouth and held one out to Jason. Carefully he pinched it between his thumb and finger, lifted it to his mouth, and swallowed it, looking steadily at Gretchen. "Ee," he said, patting the tray.

While Gretchen was lining up three more pieces of cheese for Jason on the high chair tray, she heard the garage

37

door open and close. That was Daddy. Gretchen's spirits lifted. If he was in a good mood, she could get him to act out a scene with her. Let's see, she had to keep on feeding Jason, so she should pretend to be someone with a baby— she could be the queen in *Rumpelstiltskin.* Daddy could be the little man, Rumpelstiltskin himself.

"Hi, ladies and gentleman." Her father walked in the back door, loosening his tie and dropping his briefcase beside the rocker.

"Hi, Joe," called Gretchen's mother.

Drawing herself up regally, Gretchen lifted her chin and spoke in a haughty voice. "The queen is feeding her royal child, so this is not a convenient time for her to talk to you, little man. If you come back tomorrow, I'm sure I can guess your name then."

Mr. Nichols stopped, looking puzzled. Then a gleam appeared in his eyes. He walked slowly toward Gretchen and Jason, smiling a little.

Gretchen tossed her head, trying to keep from smiling back. Daddy *was* in a good mood. Now he was thinking up something for Rumpelstiltskin to say.

Stopping a few feet from Gretchen, Mr. Nichols put his hands on his hips. "Queen, huh?" He spoke out of the corner of his mouth. "You're nothing but a miller's daughter to me, baby. If it wasn't for me, you'd be stitching up flour sacks right now, and don't forget it. The deal is, guess my name or hand over the kid, pronto."

Gretchen put her arms protectively around Jason. "No, varlet! You shall not have my child. I can still guess your name. Is it . . . Rip van Winkle?"

Her father shook his head scornfully. "Uh-uh."

38

"Da-da," said Jason, leaning over his tray toward his father.

"Jason knows," said Mrs. Nichols, watching them from the stove.

Clasping her hands, Gretchen the Queen gazed up at the rafters. "Is it . . . Rutabaga?"

"You're way off base, sister," said Mr. Nichols. "Fork over the kid."

"Well, then," said Gretchen slyly, "it must be—Rumpelstiltskin!" As his eyes widened and his mouth dropped open, she smothered a giggle.

"How did you find out?" snarled Daddy the Gnome. "I've been double-crossed. I'm gonna put my foot through the royal floor!"

But as he lifted one foot to stamp, Mrs. Nichols ran around the divider, waving a pot holder. "Please, darling —think of the carpenter's bill. We had to get a new hot-water heater just last month." She grabbed his arm.

Mr. Nichols pretended to wrestle with her. "No, come on, it's in the script. I have to stamp my foot through the floor."

Gretchen gave up trying not to laugh, and Jason crowed and rattled his tray.

"That's enough. Curtain!" Mrs. Nichols chuckled, pushing Mr. Nichols away. "Dinnertime. You set the table, Gretchen, while I make the omelets."

Opening the knives-and-forks drawer, Gretchen felt a tug in the direction of the stairs and remembered Errora again. All right, she told herself, I *will* go check—right after dinner.

In a short while they were sitting around the table, eating

their omelets. "When's your class play coming up, Gretchen?" asked her father. "You're going to be a star."

Gretchen slowly put down her fork. The play. She felt the smile on her face fading.

"Oh, yes—the play!" Mrs. Nichols leaned toward Gretchen. "I meant to ask you last night, and then I was so busy getting ready for the company, I forgot about it. Did Mrs. Sheppard assign the parts yet?"

Gretchen looked at her father, then at her mother, then down at her plate. "Yes." She was torn between not wanting to talk about it and wanting their sympathy.

"And what's your part?" asked Mr. Nichols. He buttered his roll.

"Nothing, that's what!" burst out Gretchen. "Mrs. Sheppard hates me! She picked Amy Sacher to be Polly Winsum, and she didn't give me any part at all—I'm just an understudy and *scenery manager*. That means I'm supposed to paint cardboard scenery and make papier-mâché pies."

Mr. Nichols shook his head, chewing slowly. "I don't get it, Gretchen. You're a good actor—no, really. I'm not just saying that because I'm your father. This Amy Sacher must be ready for Broadway."

Gretchen snorted. "Oh, she's terrific. This is the way Amy acts: 'I am so distressed. Boo, hoo, hoo.' " She made her voice even more flat than Amy's had actually sounded.

Mrs. Nichols put her hand on Gretchen's arm. "I'm sorry, Gretchen. You must be terribly disappointed."

Tears welled into Gretchen's eyes. She tried to speak around the lump in her throat. "It's so mean of Mrs. Sheppard! I've been looking forward to the play all this time."

"I know," said her mother. "The trouble is, I don't think

40

Mrs. Sheppard knows that. She probably doesn't even know you can act. From what she told me at the February conference, you haven't—" Mrs. Nichols hesitated, fiddling with her fork. "Mrs. Sheppard seemed to think you were—I don't know. She didn't come right out and say it, but I think your attitude bothered her." She looked questioningly at Gretchen.

"Well, *her* attitude bothers me!" exclaimed Gretchen. "Why couldn't I get Miss DiGrassi for a teacher instead of her? You should hear the way Mrs. Sheppard talks. She says, 'People' "—Gretchen pretended to push glasses up on her nose with one finger—" 'people, every part in this play is important.' She must think I'm so dumb I won't notice that Amy Sacher has the best part and I don't have any part at all!" Her voice choked on the last words.

Gretchen looked at her father for sympathy, but he was shaking his head again. "Gretchen, Gretchen. All right, so you don't like Mrs. Sheep Dog"—he grinned at Gretchen, but she didn't smile back—"very well. You can't decide to get along with just the people you like. Where would I be if I only tried to get along with the customers I liked? I'd lose half my sales, and I'd be out on my ear."

"Oh, dear." Mrs. Nichols sighed, tearing a piece of her roll into bits for Jason. "I wish I'd paid more attention to the way things were going downhill between you and Mrs. Sheppard, Gretchen. Your father's right—if you can't get along with her, you're the one who's going to suffer."

Gretchen's tears had dried up. So it was her fault, was it? Outraged, she stared from her mother to her father. She was supposed to "get along" with Mrs. Sheppard, no matter how unfair the teacher was. But of course they weren't

41

going to go to Mrs. Sheppard and lecture her about "getting along" with Gretchen.

"I think maybe you were spoiled by always having teachers you liked up until this year," her father went on. "Real life is tougher than that."

And now she was spoiled! She was not going to sit there, listening to their lectures, a minute longer. "Excuse me," she muttered, pushing back her chair.

Aware of the silence at the table behind her—her mother and father would be exchanging their grown-up glances—Gretchen carried her half-eaten omelet to the kitchen counter and set the plate down sharply. Then she swung her leg over the baby gate and stamped upstairs.

But before she reached the top of the stairs, Gretchen saw light on the carpet in the darkened hall. It was coming from her half-open bedroom door. As if someone were running a movie projector in her room.

Gretchen had forgotten about Errora.

6

A Tough Spell

"Hours late!" Errora hitched up the waistband of her baggy, drab blue skirt with an angry jerk. "The Agency closes at five o'clock, you know. What if Aunt Injuncta noticed—I mean, I have no authorization to work after hours."

"I'm sorry," said Gretchen, shutting the door behind her. She felt suddenly cheerful, even though Errora was upset with her. "I couldn't come up here before now."

"Well!" Errora snorted, then seemed to decide to let it go. "Never mind, this once." She held her Enchantulator in front of her, thumb poised over a button. "Let's record your debriefing, and then you may express your gratitude."

Express her gratitude! Gretchen started to laugh.

"Please speak clearly for the record," said Errora. "You arrived at school this morning, Amy was there with her hair cut, and—"

"And nothing," said Gretchen. "When we read the play,

44

Mrs. Sheppard said Amy was doing fine. She didn't change the parts at all."

"She didn't—" Errora's voice trailed off. She stared at the Enchantulator, fingering the keys. "But I thought I—but the solution—"

"Amy said her mother took her to have her hair cut," Gretchen went on. "I don't think your Enchantulator really did anything."

"You don't think— But this is the best Enchantulator in the Agency! It's my Aunt—" Then Errora stopped, pulled herself up straight, and adjusted the visor of her cap. "I see." Her tone was offended. "You don't possess confidence in my ability to terminate situational obstacles. All right, you can solve your own problems."

"No, wait!" said Gretchen. "I didn't mean you couldn't help me. Couldn't you try something else?"

Errora looked up at the ceiling, sucking in her plump cheeks. "Well . . . Maybe the termination of your situational obstacles can be implemented some other way." She began to tap the keys of the Enchantulator. "Problem: a certain predisposition on the part of your teacher tending toward favorable outcomes for Amy and negative outcomes for you."

No kidding, thought Gretchen.

"Solution"—Errora jabbed a key, and her face lit up— "initiate a transfer of personalities!" She beamed at Gretchen. "You see? If you were Amy, you'd be the one the teacher liked. *You'd* be the one starring in the play."

Gretchen shook her head, frowning. "That doesn't make any sense. If I were Amy, I wouldn't be me."

Errora sighed impatiently. "Well, of course you wouldn't actually *be* Amy. You'd be yourself, except in Amy's

45

body. Are the potentialities making themselves evident?"

"Oh!" Gretchen caught on. It would be like wearing a costume—a disguise. Like a gorilla suit, only it would be an Amy Sacher suit. "Everyone would think I was Amy! Even Mrs. Sheppard."

Errora nodded. "Exactly. Now, in order to concretize this concept, I'll need the pictorial representation of Amy again. And one of you, too."

Where was that picture of Amy? Gretchen found the newspaper clipping behind her dresser. Then she hesitated, struck by a thought. "Will it—will it hurt?"

Errora looked insulted. "My technique mastery has reached a high level of achievement. It is extremely unlikely that any degree of discomfort will be experienced. What about a picture of you?"

Gretchen pulled a school picture of herself from her desk drawer.

"Fine," said Errora. "Following this, we need a material object for the facilitation of the spell. That should work." She pointed to a cardboard photograph folder on Gretchen's desk with a picture of her Aunt Marianne. "Take that picture out, then glue Amy's picture on one side and yours on the other."

Gretchen got out the glue. Amy's black-and-white newspaper picture wrinkled damply as she pressed it on one side of the folder. Then Gretchen stuck her own picture, in color, opposite Amy's. With the pictures facing, she and Amy seemed to be smiling at each other, as if they were good friends. The idea gave Gretchen an odd feeling—of course she and Amy had never smiled at each other like that.

"That's quite satisfactory," said Errora, examining the

46

pictures. "They'll make contact when the folder closes, which is the key factor." She pushed up her sleeves and held out the Enchantulator. "For purposes of personal safety, please vacate the immediate vicinity."

"What?—oh." Gretchen backed up to the door and leaned against it, studying Errora with a frown. There was something strange about her—other than her drab blue suit and her calculator-wand. Although she wasn't fat, her face was very round, and her hands were plump. And maybe fairy godmothers wore uniforms nowadays, but why didn't Errora wear one that fit? And why did she talk part of the time like a normal person and part of the time in a pea-soup fog of words?

"Uhn." Errora grunted, banging at a key with her small, pudgy fist. "What a tough spell! But it goes without saying," she added, glancing at Gretchen, "that difficulties are surmounted in a competent manner by experienced fairy godmothers like me. There!" Sparks sputtered from the edge of the Enchantulator, then merged into a steady beam, spotlighting the cardboard photograph folder on Gretchen's desk.

Errora chanted, her voice rising at the end of the first and third lines:

While physical attributes remain in position,
Personality components undergo a transfer,
And a quasi-permanent state of exchange will ensue.

Watching Errora, Gretchen noticed that her eyes were opening wide, as if she were surprised—maybe dismayed. She held on to the Enchantulator with both hands, her face red with effort. As Errora pronounced the last word, the

47

Enchantulator made a fizzling noise, and its light faded.

Gretchen heard a soft *slap* from the desk. The cardboard folder was lying flat, closed.

Errora wiped her forehead with her baggy sleeve. "I— I have to address myself to the matter of my departure. I'll come back on—when did you say the play was?"

"May 7," said Gretchen. "Or is it May 8?" Then something struck her. "Hey! Nothing happened." She looked down at herself. "I'm not in Amy's body. This is me."

"What did you expect?" snapped Errora. "That spell is of significant magnitude, so of course it won't reach peak effectiveness for a couple of hours. Meanwhile, it would be inadvisable for me to continue in the presently held location. Aunt— I mean, I have to go now."

Suddenly Gretchen seemed to feel the spell working away inside her, like a ticking bomb. "Wait!" She pushed herself away from the door. "What if—if something goes wrong before May? If I want to change back to myself?"

Errora looked irritated. "How could anything go wrong? I thought I made you cognizant of my technique mastery. But the spell is triggered by the position of the folder. If you want to reverse it, just open the folder. Is that adequate amplification? See you at a future point in time."

Gretchen would have liked to go over the "amplification" again, but Errora had disappeared.

Gretchen sat down on her bed. Now she had to wait for the spell to take effect. As a matter of fact, she felt a little funny already. Her skin felt . . . tight, as if she were getting too big for it. The inside of her head felt tight, too.

Maybe she had just eaten too much for dinner. No, don't be silly. She hadn't even finished one helping. Standing up

49

to look in the mirror, Gretchen turned sideways. She smoothed her striped jersey over her stomach. She didn't *look* any fatter. Her head looked the same, too. Same freckled face, same wavy, gingery hair.

Maybe the magic would happen while Gretchen was asleep. She might as well get ready for bed. Gretchen undressed and put on her pajamas. The tight feeling was getting worse. Her head seemed to be inflating like a beach ball, and the skin all over her body felt thin and tender.

There was a knock on the door. "Gretchen?" Mr. Nichols opened the door. "Listen, I'm sorry you feel so bad about the play. It's not really—" He stopped, looking hard at Gretchen. "Good lord, are you sick? You look—strange." He stuck his head out the door and called downstairs. "Linda? Come take a look at Gretchen."

Mrs. Nichols ran up the stairs. "I don't think she has a fever," she said, feeling Gretchen's forehead. "But she does look—strange. Do you feel sick, darling?"

"I don't know." Gretchen was getting scared. She didn't know what to say—not the truth, certainly. "I—I have a sort of headache."

"Hm." Mrs. Nichols straightened up, still looking at Gretchen with concern. "I'll give you an aspirin. Maybe you're coming down with something."

A few minutes later, Gretchen was alone in her dark bedroom, wide-awake—and afraid. There was nothing for her to do but lie here, feeling stranger and stranger. Now her ears were ringing from the pressure inside her head. Gretchen turned over on her side—carefully, because her skin felt as if it could pop open any minute, like a jammed-full suitcase.

50

What if Errora hadn't cast the spell quite right? She hadn't given Gretchen any hint that she would feel like this.

What if—what if Errora wasn't a kindly fairy godmother, after all? For all Gretchen knew, Errora could be someone entirely different. Maybe a crazy scientist experimenting on girls. She had seemed sort of crazy at the beginning, Gretchen remembered.

Now Gretchen was so frightened she wanted to jump up and run downstairs to her parents. But she was more afraid of what would happen if she made a sudden move. And anyway, what could Mom or Daddy do? Gretchen had to get Errora to come back.

"Errora?" she called softly.

Nothing happened, except the top of Gretchen's skull felt as if it were going to start jumping up and down like the lid on a boiling saucepan. Then Gretchen's eyes focused on the white photograph folder lying on the desk. Why hadn't she remembered? Errora had told her how to reverse the spell: open the folder, separating her picture from Amy's.

Forgetting to be careful, Gretchen flung back the covers and swung her legs over the side of the bed.

And then Gretchen felt something split. Now she tried to scream, but it was too late. She could feel herself slipping away, a grape spurting out of its skin. For an everlasting moment, she hung in nothing—black, soundless emptiness.

Then Gretchen felt a pillow underneath her head. The bursting feeling was gone. Her skin seemed to seal itself closed again, loose and comfortable. But she could hear herself drawing loud, rasping breaths. She clutched the bedclothes, grateful to be touching something.

51

Slowly Gretchen opened her eyes. On the other side of the room, the window framed a black branch. Pressing her cheek against the pillow, Gretchen let out a long sigh. Nothing had happened after all. She felt silly for having been so frightened.

On the other hand, she was disappointed to go through all that for nothing. Since she hadn't changed places with Amy—

Wait a minute.

Gretchen sat up in bed, staring across the room at the branch outside the window. There wasn't any tree outside *her* bedroom window. Turning her head, she saw numbers glowing from the clock on the night table. That was a digital clock. But Gretchen's alarm clock had a round face.

And her pajamas—she was now wearing a nightgown. In the dark Gretchen fingered the ruffled cuffs at her wrists. Then her hands touched each other. These hands with small, slim fingers were not her hands.

Half eagerly, half fearfully, Gretchen jumped out of bed. Fumbling, she found the light switch by the door and pushed it up. Light flooded the room. Gretchen blinked at the full-length mirror on the back of the closed bedroom door.

Blinked at Amy Sacher's brown eyes.

Drawing in her breath sharply, Gretchen put her hand to her mouth. So did the reflection.

This time, Errora's spell had worked.

7

Inside Amy's Skin

When the alarm went off the next morning, Gretchen made a grumbling noise and burrowed deeper into the covers. Did she really have to get up? She hadn't slept well last night—she kept waking up and staring at the luminescent numbers on . . .

. . . Amy's clock! Eyes popping open, Gretchen sat up.

"Amy!" called a woman's voice from downstairs. "Are you getting dressed?"

Gretchen's heart raced. That must be Mrs. Sacher. How could she get out of the house without letting Mrs. Sacher see her? She would be so angry when she found out—

But she wouldn't. Would she? Scrambling out of bed, Gretchen checked in the full-length mirror again. No, Mrs. Sacher wasn't going to find out anything, because she would see just what Gretchen was seeing: Amy's large brown eyes under Amy's blonde bangs. Opening the door, she called back, "Coming!" It was Amy's voice.

53

Gretchen turned toward the closet, ignoring the uneasiness at the back of her mind. Now she would get dressed and go downstairs and go to school, and no one would suspect she wasn't Amy. Errora was right; changing places with Amy was the solution. It was fun, wasn't it? Like being a secret agent—or acting a part in a play.

As Gretchen zipped up a pair of green corduroy jeans, she caught herself thinking it was a good thing she and Amy were the same size. The same size! She laughed out loud, shaking her head at herself in the mirror. She had forgotten again already.

Picking up Amy's book bag from her desk, Gretchen peeked out into the hall. The coast was clear. Funny, she really did feel like a spy in a foreign country. Amy's mother was downstairs. Did Amy have brothers and sisters? Gretchen didn't know.

Just act normal, she told herself as she went down the stairs. No baby gate here. She followed the smell of coffee into the kitchen.

"Hi, baby."

Even though the woman sitting at the counter wore a bathrobe and no makeup, Gretchen recognized her lean face. It was the face of the woman in the newspaper with Amy. Act normal, she told herself again. Her stomach flipped.

Still reading her paper, Mrs. Sacher sipped her coffee. "The fashion page says, 'Long Hair Makes a Comeback.' I wonder if we should have—" As if remembering something, she broke off and looked up at Gretchen. "How's your headache? All gone? We've got to be at the top of our form today."

Gretchen felt uneasy with Amy's mother looking at her so closely. Was there any way she could guess? Mothers were supposed to be able to tell their own children, no matter what. "I feel great," she said, stepping back. "I'm just hungry." She thought of bacon and eggs, English muffins with marmalade.

"Good." Mrs. Sacher pointed to a bowl on the counter. "I poured your Vitaflakes for you."

Vitaflakes? It didn't sound appetizing, but—Gretchen looked at the clock on the stove—there was no time for arguing this morning. Pushing herself up onto a stool, she poured milk on the cereal and began to eat. The Vitaflakes tasted like little pieces of paper towel soaked in milk.

"Don't forget to come straight out after school," said Mrs. Sacher. "I'll be waiting in the car. If we don't leave right then, we won't get to the studio in the city by four o'clock."

Gretchen choked down a mouthful of Vitaflakes. "Why are we going there?"

"Why!" Mrs. Sacher laughed shortly. "Now, baby, pull yourself together. This isn't the day for you to be off. If they choose you for the underwear commercial—"

Gretchen's spoon dropped into her bowl, spattering milk. "Underwear!" She dabbed at Amy's sweater with her paper napkin. "But Mrs. Sacher—" Oh, no. What did Amy call her mother? Not Mrs. Sacher!

Taking Gretchen firmly by the shoulders, Mrs. Sacher looked at her even more carefully than before. "Amy Renata Sacher, you are not yourself this morning."

Gretchen looked down, wishing Mrs. Sacher's bony face weren't so close to her own.

55

"I thought I made it clear how important this audition is for your future. It could open all kinds of doors."

Gretchen said nothing. You haven't been doing a very good job of acting like Amy, she told herself. She would have to keep in mind who she was supposed to be, not just with Mrs. Sacher but at school, too.

". . . the truth, sugar baby," Amy's mother was saying. "Is that bad old headache still bothering you?"

"No, really, it's all gone," said Gretchen uncomfortably. It dawned on her that Amy must have undergone the same scary experience as Gretchen last night—only Amy wouldn't have known what in the world was happening. She felt a pang of guilt.

"All right, then, you'd better run along." Mrs. Sacher let go of Gretchen's shoulders and picked up her coffee cup.

Grabbing the book bag, Gretchen headed for the nearest door, praying she wouldn't find herself in a closet. No, thank goodness, this door led into the garage. She picked Amy's jacket from a coat tree as she went out.

Hurrying past a sleek silver gray car and out into the cool sunshine, Gretchen felt her spirits rise. It was a relief to be outside, away from Amy's bossy mother. And it was another fine almost-spring day, with a few clouds but mostly blue sky.

At the curb Gretchen wondered whether to turn right or left, but only for a moment. Either way, she would soon come to another street and a street sign, and then she would know where she was.

Sure enough, at the first intersection she found out she was on Mallard Street, which ran beside the golf course. Mallard Street would take Gretchen across the West River to Cross Street, which ran into School Street, on which, of course, was the school. She began to walk briskly, swinging the book bag.

A short while later, Gretchen slid into her seat beside Beth. Not even tardy, she thought with satisfaction. "Hi, Beth."

Beth stared at Gretchen-in-Amy. "What do you think you're doing? That's Gretchen's seat."

For a second Gretchen stared back at her friend blankly. Then she jumped up, her face hot. "Sorry. I—sorry." Bumping against a chair, she made her way to Amy's table and sat down next to Kathy. You dummy! she scolded herself. You're Amy! You have to pretend you're Amy. How could you make such a stupid mistake?

Gretchen became aware that Kathy was looking at her expectantly. "Hey, Amy—notice anything different?" When Gretchen didn't answer, Kathy shook her head, her short, dark hair flying out and settling down again. She smiled at Gretchen-in-Amy as though they shared a secret. "Twinsies."

"Oh," said Gretchen. "You got your hair cut." Twinsies! Ick.

The tardy bell rang. Mrs. Sheppard was standing in front of the class, marking the attendance book, when the classroom door swung open. Gasping for breath, a girl with messy reddish hair, wearing a familiar-looking striped jersey, leaned against the door.

Gretchen drew in her breath sharply. It was like seeing a ghost. But the other children began to giggle and whisper. Gretchen saw Kathy smile the kind of smile that meant it was fun to see someone else look silly and get into trouble.

57

Unsmiling, Mrs. Sheppard glanced toward the door. "You'll have to take a tardy slip to the office, Gretchen. Goodness me, didn't you comb your hair this morning?"

But Amy-in-Gretchen paid no attention to the teacher. Spotting Gretchen-in-Amy in her seat, she lunged toward her, stumbling around the tables. She crouched beside Gretchen so that her freckled nose was just a few inches away. "What happened?" she whispered hoarsely. "What are we going to do? Isn't it awful? They wouldn't believe me at your house. You've got to—"

Gretchen drew back. "Go sit down!" she muttered. She didn't know what to do with Amy. Why hadn't Errora warned her about this?

Amy-in-Gretchen did not go sit down or even move an inch. "But I want to get back in myself!" she wailed like a little child. Then a look of baffled rage came over her face. "Get out of me, right now! I'll—I'll just make you get right out of me!" She grabbed a handful of hair on each side of Gretchen-in-Amy's head and yanked, hard.

"Ow!" screamed Gretchen. She tried to pry Amy-in-Gretchen's hands away, but the other girl only pulled harder. "Ow!"

Then Gretchen sensed someone bending over them, and she heard two sharp smacks. Amy cried out. Feeling her hair go loose, Gretchen looked up to see Mrs. Sheppard brandishing a ruler. The teacher seized Amy-in-Gretchen by the arm.

Dragging Amy toward the door, Mrs. Sheppard hissed, "This time you have really gone too far, Gretchen Nichols. Mr. Mixell will have something to say to you, since you can't control your behavior in my classroom."

"But you don't understand!" Amy-in-Gretchen began to sob, pointing back with her free hand at Gretchen-in-Amy. "I'm not—"

The door swung closed behind them. For an instant there was shocked silence, and then an uproar of talk and laughter burst out.

But Gretchen didn't laugh. She was shaking. Cautiously she rubbed her sore scalp, but she knew that was the least of her problems. Amy was not going to cooperate. She was making such a fuss about finding herself in Gretchen's body that either someone would start to believe her or they would lock her up in the nut house.

Either way, Gretchen would be in big trouble.

"Hey, Amy, you know what I think?" Kathy leaned over confidentially. "I think Gretchen's jealous of you."

"She is not!" said Gretchen. Then she added hastily, "I don't know what's the matter with her." Gretchen didn't want to talk to Kathy. She had to think.

Could she somehow get to Amy, persuade her that changing bodies was fun, like going away to summer camp? She should have done that beforehand. Why hadn't Errora thought of that? Maybe Errora could have put a little extra charm in the spell to make Amy think she was having a super adventure.

Mrs. Sheppard stalked back into the classroom. "People! People! When I leave the room, I expect you to behave just as if I were here. My second graders had better manners than this. Book monitor, pass out the reading books, and everyone read *quietly.* The assignments are on the board. Amy, I'd like to talk to you privately for a moment, please."

With cold in the pit of her stomach, Gretchen-in-Amy stepped up to the teacher's desk. Had Mrs. Sheppard found out somehow—had she finally believed Amy-in-Gretchen's story?

But the teacher was gazing at her sympathetically through her pink glasses. "Are you all right, dear? Would you like to go to the nurse's office to rest for a little while?"

"No—I'm fine, really," mumbled Gretchen. "She just pulled my hair a little."

Mrs. Sheppard took Gretchen-in-Amy's hand and squeezed it. "My dear, I'm so sorry you had to suffer such an attack from that—that undisciplined child. I just wanted to explain to you, in case you blamed yourself in any way, that she has emotional problems."

What a thing for the teacher to say! "No, she doesn't!" Then Gretchen caught herself. "I mean—"

Mrs. Sheppard squeezed her hand again. "You don't understand, Amy. I'm sure this is beyond your experience. But when a child acts the way Gretchen acted just now, something is very wrong. In my opinion, she may need professional help—maybe there is a problem at home. But *you* needn't worry about that."

That's what you think, said Gretchen silently, going back to her seat.

It was a tiring morning for Gretchen. She couldn't relax for a second, or she'd forget and do something dumb like joining the wrong reading group.

Besides, Gretchen was worrying about what had happened to Amy-in-Gretchen. The principal couldn't be talking to her all this time. He must have called Gretchen's mother to come and take her "emotional-problem" child home.

Oh, no. Mom would have to leave her office to pick up

61

Amy-in-Gretchen. Would she drop her off at Mrs. Terrence's Play-Care Center, where Jason stayed while Gretchen was in school?

No. Mrs. Terrence wouldn't want to look after a crazy-acting fifth grader. Mom would have to take Amy home and stay with her all day. What would Amy say? Could she make Mom believe she wasn't really Gretchen?

The uneasiness Gretchen had felt earlier grew into foreboding. This wasn't what she had meant to happen at all. Why hadn't Errora arranged things better?

It was a relief when lunchtime came. But halfway to the cafeteria, Gretchen realized she didn't have any lunch money. Luckily Beth always had extra money, and there were her braids ahead of Gretchen in line.

"Beth?" said Gretchen. "I forgot my lunch money. Could you lend me fifty cents?"

Beth's braids flew out as she whipped around. For the second time that morning, she gave Gretchen-in-Amy an unfriendly stare. "Me lend you fifty cents? After you got Gretchen sent to the principal? I hope you starve." She turned her back.

At least I have a really true friend, thought Gretchen glumly. Too bad she isn't any use right now, since she thinks I'm Amy. Dropping back in line, she spotted Kathy. Kathy would lend Amy lunch money, if she had any extra.

As Gretchen thought, Kathy was pleased to lend her fifty cents. "Want to come over to my house after school?"

Gretchen looked at her in irritation. She supposed Amy would say yes, but Gretchen didn't feel like spending the afternoon with Kathy. Then she remembered. "Gee, I'm really sorry, I can't. My mother's picking me up from

62

school. I have to go to a TV audition in the city." She put her tray down at their table.

Kathy's eyes were round with admiration. "You're going to be on TV? What program?"

"No, it's not like that," said Gretchen through a mouthful of Turkey Bites. "It's just a commercial. And I might not even get picked—this is just a tryout."

"Oh, I bet you'll get it!" Kathy leaned across the table to the other girls. "Guess what! Amy's going to be on TV!"

"No, I'm not!" said Gretchen-in-Amy.

But it was too late. The other girls wanted to know all about it. Of course Gretchen couldn't tell them much, and they thought she was teasing them by holding out. The only one who didn't ask any questions was Beth, at the other end of the table. Beth gazed at her in an unfriendly way, eating steadily.

When the babble had died down, Beth said in a loud, deliberate voice, "What *kind* of a commercial, Amy?"

How could Beth know it was something embarrassing? Gretchen-in-Amy pushed a Turkey Bite around her plate with a celery stick. "I don't really—um—"

"I bet it's something stupid," said Beth in the same loud voice. "Like dog food. I bet they dress you up in a dog suit and you eat dog food."

"Shut up, Beth," said Kathy. "You don't know anything about it."

"Neither do you," shot back Beth. "And by the way, you look pretty silly with your hair cut just like Amy's. You probably think you'll get to be a model, too."

Sucking milk noisily through her straw, Gretchen looked around the cafeteria for something to distract them. "Hey!"

she said, pointing to the next table. "Look at Dennis!"

Good old Dennis. You could always count on him for entertainment. He had put a glob of peanut butter on the end of a straw wrapper, still half on his straw, and he was aiming the straw like a peashooter at the ceiling. As the girls turned to watch, Dennis's cheeks puffed out and the straw cover hurtled into the air. Not quite as far as the ceiling, though—it dropped back down onto the head of the boy next to Dennis.

Then Dennis and the other boy started punching each other, and the teacher on lunch duty hurried over to their table, and then the end-of-lunch bell was ringing. Gretchen sighed with relief. No more questions about her commercial.

After recess Gretchen remembered they were going to start rehearsing the play with Miss DiGrassi this afternoon. A thrill of pleasure went through her. The play was what she had gone to all this trouble for, after all. Taking Amy's copy of the script from her shelf under the table, she turned the pages. Amy had marked Polly Winsum's lines in pink crayon. But pink or yellow, they were Gretchen's lines now.

And somehow Gretchen didn't feel so worried anymore about what Amy might do. Sure, she was upset this morning. Who wouldn't be? But probably she would settle down now and make the best of being stuck in Gretchen's body for a while. She had to see that no one was going to believe she was actually Amy. Or maybe she would just decide that she *was* Gretchen and had gotten confused.

The afternoon went along smoothly until it was time for gym, and the actors in the play were sent to Miss DiGrassi's classroom. Miss DiGrassi, a thin, energetic woman with wiry gray hair, had them sit in a circle with her.

"I'm looking forward to working with you on *Polly's Pies in Peril,*" she said. "We're going to have a lot of fun, and we're going to put on a terrific show. Okay. We're just going to read through the script this afternoon. Next week we'll start rehearsing in the gym, every Wednesday after school. Can you all come to rehearsals that day? Good. All right. What is acting?" Miss DiGrassi looked around the circle.

The girl who was playing the mother said, "It's pretending to be someone else."

The teacher nodded. "Good. I'd add something more to that—I'd say it's actually getting into someone else's skin."

In shock, Gretchen stared at the teacher. Could Miss DiGrassi know? Then she shook herself. Don't be silly. Miss DiGrassi was just using an expression.

They began reading the play aloud. In the middle of the first scene, Miss DiGrassi said, "Good! We're off to a terrific start. I like the way you're reading with expression, especially Amy—it is Amy, isn't it?"

For a frozen moment, Gretchen was sure Miss DiGrassi suspected something. Then she sat up straight. "Yes, I'm Amy," she said firmly. "Amy Sacher." Miss DiGrassi was just complimenting her, that was all. Gretchen would do a much better job as Polly Winsum than the real Amy could. Which just showed that Errora's idea of changing bodies had been the right solution, didn't it?

Only—Gretchen wished she didn't have to explain to herself why it was all right.

8

A Change of Heart

Jostled by the crowd of children in the hall, Gretchen looked wistfully at Beth's brown braids disappearing through the double doors. She and Beth usually walked partway home together. Of course Beth wouldn't want to walk with her today, believing that she was Amy.

Through the windows in the doors Gretchen caught sight of cars lined up at the curb. Mothers picking up kids. Then she stopped just inside the doors. She had recognized one of the cars at the curb, a sleek, silver gray, two-door car. She could even see Amy's sleek mother at the wheel, watching the children streaming out of the school. Waiting for her.

Abruptly Gretchen whirled and started fighting her way back through the crowd. "Watch it!" said a boy. "Ow— look where you're going!" said a little girl. A teacher standing against the wall warned, "No shoving, please!" But Gretchen, intent on the red EXIT sign over the back door, only struggled harder. Someone said, "You're not supposed to go out that way, Amy." Gretchen threw herself against the long door handle.

Free of the crowd at last, she staggered onto the pavement. There was no one on the playground. Gretchen's feet pounded over the foursquare chalk marks on the asphalt, thudded across the playing field. Amy's book bag bumped against her legs.

At the edge of the field, she plunged into the leafless woods. Briers tore at her jeans and jacket, and a branch whipped her cheek, but she crashed on through the bushes and saplings.

And then Gretchen found herself standing, chest heaving, on a path. It was the nature walk path, the one that led to the marsh.

Slowly Gretchen took one step, then another. What was the matter with her? She wasn't being reasonable. She couldn't run away! Mrs. Sacher was waiting for her. She had to turn around, walk down the path to the edge of the woods and across the playing field and the asphalt and back through the school, out the front door, and climb into the sleek silver gray car with her sleek mother. It was just part of the game of pretending to be Amy.

"No!" The word burst from Gretchen's lips. She felt almost sick. She couldn't even pretend Mrs. Sacher was her mother. A bony-faced mother who wanted her daughter to be in an underwear commercial? Never! *Mother* meant Mom.

The path reached a stream with a plank across it. Stepping onto the plank, Gretchen felt it flex under her weight. Downstream the woods gave way to marshy fields, where

67

wind blew across the winter-bleached reeds. Shivering, Gretchen pulled up the zipper on her jacket. Amy's jacket.

Gretchen looked down at the hand on the zipper. Amy's slim-fingered hand. She swallowed hard. She missed her own wide hands. No—she didn't just *miss* them. What she felt was stronger than that. Like wearing someone else's damp bathing suit, only a hundred times worse.

Gretchen saw the weeks stretching out ahead of her like a prison term: the rest of March, all of April, the first part of May. Why had she thought she could stand being someone else all that time?

Looking up, as if for an answer, she saw that the sky above the marsh and woods had clouded over. Not a ray of sunshine or a patch of blue—just cold, blank gray. The day had slipped backwards from spring to winter.

With her next thought, the cold seemed to reach Gretchen's heart. What if she couldn't change back after the play was over? What if Errora didn't return?

But Errora had said Gretchen could reverse the spell herself, just by opening the photo folder on her desk.

But what if something happened to the folder? What if Amy tossed it into the wastebasket, which she emptied into the trash barrel, which Gretchen's father then carted off to the dump? The folder would be crushed and lost forever in the trash compactor.

That did it. It didn't matter what else happened—Gretchen had to get home today. This afternoon. Right now!

As if a rope tying her to Mrs. Sacher had snapped, Gretchen leaped from the plank to the other side of the stream and began to trot along the path through gray blond clumps of marsh grass. This path should come out onto

Campground Drive, which ran into West River Road, which led back to the flagpole at the center of town. From the flagpole she would walk home the way she always did, up Maple Avenue, past the Congregational church to Thatcher Lane.

Walk? It was all Gretchen could do to keep herself from breaking into a gallop.

Loping past the pine trees along Campground Drive, Gretchen heard a car engine slowing behind her. Out of the corner of her eye, she saw the car pulling up to the curb. Her heart flipped. Run for your life!

But no—it wasn't a silver two-door car, but a blue station wagon. The driver, a woman Gretchen vaguely recognized, was rolling down the window. "Amy?" she called. "Is something the matter?"

She must be a neighbor of Amy's or a friend of Amy's mother. Gretchen had better answer her. "No," she said, panting. "I'm—I'm just going to visit a friend."

"Where does your friend live?"

What a nosy woman! Gretchen felt a flash of anger, but she answered politely. "Thatcher Lane."

"My goodness, that's a long walk, even for your young legs." Leaning across the seat, the woman opened the car door. "Hop in. I'll give you a ride—I'm going near there, anyway."

Gretchen didn't know how to get out of it. Anyway, she realized, as she sank into the car seat, she *was* out of breath, and her legs *were* trembling. Maybe it would be all right. She just had to be careful how she answered the woman's questions, that was all.

But the driver only chatted about the weather and how beautifully groomed Amy's mother always looked. In a few minutes the blue station wagon had passed the white-stee-pled church and was turning onto Thatcher Lane. "Say!" the woman exclaimed. "I bet you're visiting Linda Nichols' little girl. Is that right?"

"Yes," said Gretchen shortly.

"Well, I'm not surprised you're pals. She's a sharp little thing, just like you."

Ick! thought Gretchen. I'm not like Amy at all. Thank goodness the ride was over. "There's my—there's Gretchen's house, where those big spruce trees are. Thanks, Mrs.—thank you very much." Forcing a smile to make up for not knowing the woman's name, she jumped out of the car.

She was home. Not Amy Sacher's house, but real home, with Mom and Jason and— Gretchen stopped stock-still in the middle of the driveway. And Amy, perfectly disguised as Gretchen. Gretchen-in-Amy couldn't just walk into this house as if she lived there.

Glancing over her shoulder, Gretchen saw the woman peering at her in the rearview mirror of the blue station wagon, driving very slowly. Gretchen smiled and waved. Go away, she said silently. Finally the station wagon reached Maple Avenue and disappeared around the corner.

Now Gretchen had to do some planning. She stepped behind a spruce tree, in case her mother came out to get the mail or something.

Peeking through the spruce needles at the bay window of the kitchen, Gretchen thought hard. In order to change back to her own body, she had to get up to her bedroom and open the cardboard folder. Should she just walk in the back door, or should she ring the bell?

Either way, it would look strange. What excuse could

Amy Sacher give for visiting Gretchen Nichols, when they didn't even like each other? And Mom knew they didn't.

A pencil. She would say that "Gretchen" had borrowed a pencil from her. Then—she didn't know what she would do next. Somehow she would get up to her bedroom. Taking a deep breath, Gretchen brushed through the spruce branches, crossed the driveway and the lawn, and climbed the steps to the back door. She rang the doorbell.

Opening the door, Mrs. Nichols raised her eyebrows politely. "Hello."

It was all Gretchen could do to keep herself from crying "Mom!" and flinging herself into her mother's arms. But she had to stay cool so that she could get upstairs. "Hi," she heard herself saying brightly. "I just came by to get a pencil Gretchen borrowed from me."

"Well—I don't know." Her mother looked worried, Gretchen noticed. There was a tense line between her eyes. "Gretchen isn't feeling too well today. She had to come home from school this morning. I guess you can get your pencil, as long as you understand you can't stay." She stepped aside.

Quickly, eagerly, Gretchen walked past the coatrack, through the laundry room. Home! There was the kitchen table, with yellow forsythia in a jug. And there was Jason sitting on the floor by the sofa, plump legs sticking straight out, and—

And kneeling in front of him, Amy-in-Gretchen, holding out Gretchen's own hands to play patty-cake. With Gretchen's own baby brother!

Gretchen forgot about staying cool. With a choking cry, she dropped Amy's book bag and charged across the kitchen, past the table, past Amy and Jason's open-mouthed

stares. "Getting my pencil!" she gasped over her shoulder. She vaulted over the baby gate and pounded up the stairs, two at a time.

"Just a minute!" called Mrs. Nichols after her. Gretchen heard her say in a lower voice, "Who *is* that girl, Gretchen?"

Amy answered in Gretchen's voice, angry and bewildered, "It's Amy Sacher."

Plunging into her bedroom, Gretchen slammed the door and locked it. For a moment she leaned against the door, her sides heaving. But there was no time to lose—Mom would certainly come after her to find out what "that girl" was doing.

The folder. Turning from the door, Gretchen saw it still lying on her desk. She began to tremble. If it had been thrown away or lost . . . never mind that now.

Gretchen heard the doorknob jiggling, and then there was a knock. "What are you doing, Amy?" Mrs. Nichols' voice was sharp. "Please come out."

Then Gretchen heard Amy say, with a note of hope in her voice, "I don't think she'll hurt anything. She's just getting her pencil."

"Just getting—" Mrs. Nichols sounded indignant. "Don't be absurd. Isn't that the girl you had a fight with this morning? I'm going to get the nail scissors."

Nail scissors, to slip into the doorknob and turn the lock! Lunging for the picture folder, Gretchen fumbled with the edges, then opened it wide.

Nothing happened.

Gretchen was still standing beside her desk. Looking down at herself, she saw Amy's green corduroy jeans. The

73

fingers holding the folder were Amy's slim fingers. "Er-rora!" Gretchen gave a sob. Errora had told her the spell would reverse. It had to.

But nothing happened.

Outside in the hall, Mrs. Nichols was saying, "Where *are* my nail scissors? Did you borrow them, Gretchen? Never mind. I'll go down to the kitchen and get a paring knife."

Gretchen's breathing was shallow and rapid. Would the spell in reverse take as long as it had last night? With desperate longing, she stared at her school picture, at her own wavy, reddish hair and freckled nose.

Her skin tightened. It was starting to work!

Then her heart leaped into her throat. Her mother's voice at the door again—and she must have the paring knife to unlock the door. "I just hope she hasn't done anything crazy, like wrecking up your room. Or hurting herself."

If Mom came into the room now, she might take the folder away from Gretchen-in-Amy and close it, and then Gretchen would be stuck. Gretchen's frantic glance flicked around the room, thinking where to hide the folder.

No—she had to stop Mom from coming in! Gretchen dashed to the door and braced herself against it.

No, hide the folder first!

But there was a clicking noise in the doorknob. Feeling the door tremble as Mom tried to open it, Gretchen pushed it shut with all her might.

And then Gretchen felt herself splitting open like an overcooked hot dog. Then the terrifying Nothing feeling.

And then Gretchen was standing just outside her bedroom, holding Jason's plump weight in her arms. In front of her, Mom stood in the open doorway. And beyond Mom, Amy (Amy-in-Amy!) sprawled backwards on the

74

rug. Thankfully Gretchen squeezed Jason until he grunted like a little pig.

"Amy!" Mrs. Nichols dropped to her knees beside the other girl. "Are you all right? Please calm down. Don't cry." She put an arm around Amy, helping her to her feet. "Here's a tissue. What's the matter?"

Wiping her face and blowing her nose, Amy let out a shuddering sigh. "I'm sorry, Mrs. Nichols. I—I don't know what got into me."

Gretchen watched her with anxiety. How could Amy explain what had just happened, especially when she didn't know? Gretchen had to help her get out of this fix. "Did you find your pencil, Amy?"

"Pencil?" Amy glared at Gretchen, her voice trembling. Gretchen expected her to shout "Why did you do this to me?" But then Amy glanced at Mrs. Nichols, and her face smoothed over as if she had slipped on a mask. She turned toward the pencil holder on the desk. "Oh, *there's* my pencil." She plucked out the one with the tuft of orange fluff on the end.

Gretchen's favorite pencil! Gretchen opened her mouth to protest, then shut it. A pencil was a small price to pay for being herself again.

"I'm sorry I bothered you, Mrs. Nichols." Amy's voice shook only a little. " 'Bye, Gretchen." For an instant, as Amy's eyes met Gretchen's, the polite mask slipped. Gretchen saw with surprise that Amy was not just angry— she was hurt, too. Then Amy looked away, moving quickly to the door. "I'd better go now."

Gretchen stepped aside for her. Amy had a lot of poise, she had to admit that.

But Mrs. Nichols hurried down the stairs behind Amy.

"Just a minute. I can't let you go home by yourself. Please wait a minute while I call your mother."

"Oh, Amy's mother isn't home," called Gretchen from the top of the stairs. "She was going to pick her up at school this afternoon." She hoped the reminder would help Amy.

Mrs. Nichols shot a puzzled glance over her shoulder at Gretchen. "How would you know—" Then the doorbell rang, and she went to answer it.

"Sugar!" shrieked another woman's voice. Gretchen stepped into the kitchen in time to see Mrs. Sacher throw her arms around Amy. "Baby! I was so worried. I would have called the police if I hadn't run into Gloria Judson, and she told me she dropped you off here." Then she held Amy at arm's length, looking at her reproachfully. "Amy, how *could* you forget about the audition?"

Amy turned her head away from her mother, staring at the floor. "I'm sorry, Mother. I was thinking so hard about going to Gretchen's and getting my—"

"Mrs. Sacher," interrupted Mrs. Nichols, "I think you should realize something strange is going on here. I had to leave work and pick Gretchen up at school this morning because she and Amy had a fight. I'm surprised Mr. Mixell didn't call you about it, too. Then just now Amy burst into our house like a wild thing and—"

"A fight?" Mrs. Sacher's voice trembled with horror. "You mean your daughter attacked mine—physically?" She lifted Amy's chin tenderly. "Your cheek! She didn't scratch your face, did she, sugar?"

Wouldn't it be funny if Mrs. Sacher knew Amy attacked her own beautiful self? Gretchen thought.

"I just scratched it on a branch or something, Mother."

Amy pulled her chin away. "I'm fine. Can't we go now?"

"Yes, I think you'd better take Amy home," said Mrs. Nichols. Her voice was tight with anger. "Amy must have been overtired—under some kind of a strain, to act like this." Stalking to the back door, she held it open.

Mrs. Sacher looked from Gretchen to her mother, eyes narrowed. "Of course we're leaving. But don't assume you've heard the last of this. Amy has just missed a very important opportunity in her career, and if I find out your daughter was the cause of it—"

"Good-*bye.*" Mrs. Nichols looked angrier than Gretchen had ever seen her.

As soon as the door closed behind Amy and Mrs. Sacher, Gretchen set Jason down and sprang into her mother's arms. "Mom! I'm so glad to be— I mean, I love you!" Her mother felt nice and soft, as always.

Mrs. Nichols hugged Gretchen back, but then she pulled away a little and gave her a bewildered look. "Why this sudden love? You've been so standoffish all day—and that weird outburst at breakfast time—and fighting with Amy at school—what is going on? Something strange is happening, I know that."

"Amy *was* acting weird, wasn't she?" Gretchen snuggled up to her mother again. Let her ask all the questions she wanted to—Gretchen didn't care.

But Mrs. Nichols didn't ask any more questions. "I guess I should start dinner," she said in a dazed voice. Moving slowly, she began to take pans and packages and cans out of the kitchen cupboards.

9

More Trouble

For a moment Gretchen wondered whether her mother was all right. But she was so glad to be herself again, she couldn't feel really worried. Everything would settle down in a little while. Happily wiggling her own fingers, Gretchen skipped back up to her room to make sure her things were in order.

The photograph folder was lying open on the floor. Probably the magic was gone from it, but just in case, Gretchen tore off the newspaper picture of Amy and the school picture of herself, taking care to keep them from touching, and slipped her Aunt Marianne's picture back in. Then she threw the picture of Amy in the wastebasket and put her own picture back in the desk.

When she went back downstairs, her mother was cooking tomato sauce and wide noodles, while Jason clutched at her legs. "Lasagne, yum," said Gretchen, leaning against the counter.

But Mrs. Nichols didn't look up. "Take Jason over there"—she motioned across the divider with her elbow—"and play with him, will you? I'm going to pour the boiling water off the noodles now, and I don't want him around." Her voice sounded strained.

Gretchen scooped Jason up and carried him around the divider, sitting down on the floor near the sofa. She began to play the Face Game with him. "Where's Gretchen's nose?" He poked her nose with a fat finger. "Right! Where's Gretchen's chin?"

As he poked her chin, the phone beside the refrigerator rang. Mrs. Nichols picked it up. "Hello? . . . Mrs. Probola? Oh, yes, the school counselor . . . Emotional problems? Mrs. Sheppard said that?" There was indignation in her voice. "Yes, I'd be glad to come talk to you, because . . . Fine, nine o'clock tomorrow."

Gretchen was listening hard, forgetting about Jason. Mrs. Probola, the school counselor? There was going to be more trouble. Gretchen felt a sinking feeling in her stomach.

Jason squealed, waving a hand in front of her face. She turned back to him and let him point to Gretchen's cheek, Gretchen's hair, Gretchen's mouth. If she didn't change the game, Gretchen's eyes would be next. "Okay, let's do it the other way. Where's Jason's ear? Right! Where's Jason's—"

There was a crash and a *splat* in the other end of the kitchen, and a cry from Mrs. Nichols. Gretchen leaped to her feet and ran around the divider. Her mother stood in front of the open oven door, staring at the red orange sauce oozing over the floor, over noodles and white curds of ricotta cheese and the shining splinters of the glass lasagne pan.

"I have had it."

Her mother was staring at the mess on the floor, but Gretchen was afraid she was thinking about something else. "I'll clean it up, Mom."

"You certainly will not touch that broken glass." Mrs. Nichols seemed to pull herself together with an effort. "Just get the baby out of here." She pointed to Jason, who had crawled past Gretchen and was patting his hand in the edge of the pool of sauce.

Grabbing a paper towel, Gretchen hauled Jason back near the sofa again, wiped his hand, and began to play patty-cake with him. But her heart wasn't in it. She listened to the pieces of the lasagne pan clinking in the wastebasket.

When Mr. Nichols came whistling in the door a little while later, Mrs. Nichols met him with her coat on. "I'm going to pick up pizza for dinner. Don't even ask."

The door closed behind her. Mr. Nichols turned his bewildered gaze to Gretchen, sitting on the sofa and pretending to read a book. Picking at the cording on the sofa cushions, she looked sideways at him. Here came the questions. Daddy was going to think she was a real jerk. Her stomach sank again.

At nine o'clock the next morning, Gretchen and her mother sat down on the hard bench outside the adjustment counselor's office. A few latecomers scurried by on their way to their classrooms, giving them curious glances.

To avoid meeting their eyes, Gretchen twisted around and studied the sign taped on the frosted glass of the door. ADJUSTMENT COUNSELOR. ADJUSTMENT made Gretchen think of tinkering with a screwdriver and a wrench, the way her mother had adjusted the seat of her bicycle last summer.

They sat in silence. Mrs. Nichols picked some lint from her suit. She looked at her watch. She crossed her legs, uncrossed them, and crossed them again the other way.

Then a woman in a dark skirt came out of the teachers' room down the hall, carrying a mug of coffee. She smiled, but her eyes were intent. "Mrs. Nichols? I'm Deborah Probola, the adjustment counselor." They shook hands. "Hello, Gretchen. Mrs. Nichols, I'd like to talk with you first, then Gretchen."

The frosted-glass door closed behind Mrs. Nichols and the adjustment counselor. Gretchen imagined the counselor lifting a giant wrench from a pegboard in her office and fitting it around her mother's head. "Now, if you'll just hold still, Mrs. Nichols . . ."

Of course, Gretchen was the one who needed adjusting, not her mother. At least, the counselor would think Gretchen needed adjusting, because Mrs. Probola had no idea what had really happened.

But maybe there *is* something wrong with me, thought Gretchen. How could I think I could change bodies with Amy without upsetting anyone, especially Amy and me?

Gretchen heard the door at the end of the hall clang, and then she saw a woman and a girl walking toward her, the woman's high heels clicking angrily. It was Amy and her mother.

Meeting Amy's reproachful stare, Gretchen wished she could explain to her that the messed-up magic was Errora's fault, that Gretchen hadn't really meant to make life hard for Amy. She couldn't explain, but at least she could say something friendly. "Hi, A—"

At Mrs. Sacher's tigerlike glare, Gretchen's greeting died

81

in her throat. Amy and her mother sat down on the bench, Mrs. Sacher placing herself between Amy and Gretchen.

The three of them sat in silence. Mrs. Sacher crossed her legs. Her foot twitched back and forth, like the tail of a cat about to pounce. Gretchen edged down the bench, away from Amy's mother.

The frosted-glass door opened, and Mrs. Nichols came out. She and Mrs. Sacher glanced at each other, then looked away. It was the first time Gretchen had ever seen her mother not speaking to someone.

"Mrs. Sacher?" asked Mrs. Probola from the doorway. "And Amy? How are you?" She smiled at them. "It'll be just a few minutes. Gretchen, please come in. Mrs. Nichols, thanks very much. I'll give you a call later today."

As Gretchen stood up, Mrs. Nichols cast a worried look at her. "Goodbye, darling. I'll be at my office if—if you need me."

Gretchen ducked under Mrs. Probola's arm. " 'Bye, Mom." She wished her mother hadn't talked to her like that in front of other people.

Of course there was no pegboard of adjusting tools in the counselor's office. There was a file cabinet and bookshelves and a chair beside the desk. Mrs. Probola made a motion for Gretchen to sit down.

Leaning back in her chair, the counselor said, "I guess you were pretty disappointed when Amy got the part you wanted in the play."

Mom must have told her that. "Yes," said Gretchen.

"Angry enough to hit somebody?" The counselor toyed with her coffee mug, as if the answer didn't matter much.

But Gretchen knew better. It was the same question her father had asked her, with disbelief in his voice, last night.

"I guess so." They must all think she was a brat. "But it wasn't Amy's fault."

Mrs. Probola looked puzzled, but she went on, "Then if Amy's not to blame, there must be someone else you're angry with." Her head to one side, the counselor regarded Gretchen intently. "I wonder . . . I just wonder who that could be, Gretchen. Someone else you're *really* angry with."

Gretchen was silent for a moment, looking down at her lap. Was it all right to tell Mrs. Probola how angry she was at Mrs. Sheppard? How unfair the teacher was? Grown-ups usually stuck together. But the adjustment counselor was nodding encouragingly. Taking a deep breath, Gretchen said, "It's—"

"—your baby brother, isn't it?" Mrs. Probola nodded again. "I can't blame you. After all, you had your mother and father's undivided attention before he came along."

Gretchen could not speak. How humiliating! How insulting! Did Mrs. Probola think she was a three-year-old, jealous of a little baby? "Jason?" she finally exclaimed. "I take *care* of Jason. He's just a baby."

The counselor was still nodding. "Of course these bad feelings are very hard to admit to. But that doesn't make them go away. You see, Gretchen, angry feelings are like water rushing through a hose. If you stop up the end of the hose, it'll spring a leak somewhere else."

Right now Gretchen's angry feelings were leaking out in the direction of Mrs. Probola. But she kept her mouth shut. Mrs. Probola's explanation made Gretchen look even more like a spoiled brat, but at least it was an explanation. It would stop them from asking more questions.

84

"Things are different at your house than they used to be, aren't they?" the counselor was saying. "When you come home in the afternoon and want to talk to your mother, the baby's always there." Mrs. Probola gazed sympathetically into Gretchen's eyes.

Her face burning, Gretchen looked down. She hated Mrs. Probola, prying into the Nichols' private lives. She wanted to shout, "You don't know anything about it!"

"Well." The adjustment counselor stood up. "It's not easy to take a look inside and find out what's really going on. But I'll bet it's a relief to get it out into the open. How old is your baby brother—nine months?"

Gretchen pushed herself out of the chair. "Eleven months," she muttered.

Mrs. Probola smiled such a sickening, kindly smile that Gretchen turned her head aside. "Eleven months is a long time to keep feelings bottled up inside you. If you want to talk some more later, I'm always here, Gretchen." She opened the door. "Mrs. Sacher?"

Amy's mother rose from the bench, giving Gretchen a hard look. "I'd rather not leave my daughter alone with this girl, after what happened."

"Gretchen is going straight to her classroom now," said Mrs. Probola calmly. "Please come in, Mrs. Sacher."

Taking the hint, Gretchen started to walk toward the stairs. But as soon as the office door closed, she heard Amy whisper, "Gretchen."

Gretchen turned to see Amy leaning forward from the bench, holding out something orange and fluffy.

"Here. Your pencil."

Walking back toward Amy, Gretchen reached out to take

85

the pencil. Then she drew her hand back. "No. I—you keep it."

"But it's yours," said Amy with a note of exasperation.

Gretchen looked down at the floor and scuffed her foot back and forth. She wanted to say something to Amy—but what could she say? "I'm sorry about— Oh, just keep the pencil!" Whirling, she ran down the hall to the stairs.

10

The Cruelest Month

During the next weeks, Gretchen felt like a turtle, either plodding along or drawn back into her shell. At first she wouldn't even play with the other girls at recess. She was sure they were whispering to each other that she was emotionally disturbed because her mother paid too much attention to her baby brother. That kind of thing always got around. Anyway, they had all seen, or thought they had seen, Gretchen attacking Amy like a crazy person.

Finally Beth persuaded her to join in the foursquare games, but still Gretchen would hardly speak to the others.

At home the only person who acted normal was Jason. Gretchen's mother and father must have believed Mrs. Probola's explanation. Now whenever Daddy picked Jason up to bounce him, he would suddenly seem to remember something. He would put Jason down and give Gretchen a squeeze. And if Mom said to Jason, "What a big boy, drinking from a cup!" she would hastily turn to Gretchen with, "I like the way you set the table without being reminded."

The worst thing was that Gretchen couldn't tell them to stop it.

Gretchen couldn't forget about the play, either. Every Wednesday after school she had to go down to the gym for rehearsal. "I can't take the time to rehearse you understudies unless someone in the main cast is absent," said Miss DiGrassi. "But that doesn't mean you don't have to pay attention. If we do need you, you'll have to know your lines."

The other understudies fidgeted and whispered, but Gretchen sat on the gym floor with her eyes fixed on the stage. She knew Polly Winsum's lines, all right—soon she knew every line in the play. She felt like a little kid without any money, pressing her nose against a candy shop window.

One day in April the class pictures were delivered, and Mrs. Sheppard passed them out just before the dismissal bell. Memories Are Made of This, it said on the envelope.

Why would I want to remember the worst year of my entire life? wondered Gretchen. She pushed the picture into her book bag unopened.

At home Mrs. Nichols was hunched over the kitchen table, sorting through piles of canceled checks, while Jason played with her shoelaces. "April is the cruelest month," she muttered as Gretchen came in.

"It is?" asked Gretchen, startled. Maybe her mother understood the way she was feeling.

"Hello, darling." Mrs. Nichols looked up and smiled at Gretchen. "Just a joke about income taxes. How was your day?"

"Fine," said Gretchen without enthusiasm. "Do you have any aluminum foil pie pans I could bring to school? We're making papier-mâché pies for the play."

"Oh, the play." Mrs. Nichols' worried eyes searched Gretchen's face. "I guess so. I'll see in a minute." Then her glance fell on Jason, toddling away from the table with a stray check clutched in his fist. "Grab that from Jay, will you?"

After retrieving the check, Gretchen climbed over the baby gate and trudged up the stairs to her room. "April is the cruelest month," she said out loud, dropping her book bag beside her desk. It fell over, and the class picture slid out. Memories Are Made of This. She shoved it, still unopened, into her bottom desk drawer.

Now it was the third Wednesday in April. "It's shaping up!" Miss DiGrassi stood in front of the stage with her hands on her hips, her face shining pink. The children who were playing the townspeople looked down at her with pleased smiles. "That's what I call working together," she went on. "All right. Amy and Dennis, let's go over the last part of scene 1 again. Mrs. McEvoy"—she turned toward Beth's mother at the piano—"can you give us the villain's entrance chords?"

Sitting cross-legged on the gym floor, Gretchen watched Miss DiGrassi guide Amy and Dennis through scene 1. Amy spoke toward the audience now, and she knew all her lines, but her face stayed as stiff and blank as a Barbie doll's.

"Remember what we talked about the first time we read the script?" asked Miss DiGrassi urgently. "Getting into your character's skin? I know you can do it, Amy. You had so much feeling in your voice that first day."

Amy's face went even blanker, but she nodded. Gretchen shivered, looking away from the stage. She wished the teacher hadn't said that.

"And Dennis—speak up! I know you have a fine loud voice, because I hear you shouting to your friends in the hall."

Dennis grinned grudgingly. He shouted the next few lines, but then his voice sank back down to a mumble. On his way offstage, he pretended to hook a basketball shot at the basket hanging in front of the curtain.

Finally it was the first Wednesday in May, the day of the last regular rehearsal. When Gretchen left for school in the morning, she noticed all the branches of the spruces beside the driveway were tipped with new needles, pale green against the dark old needles. Everything is new and fresh, she thought. The oak branches hanging over the lane had put out tender pink leaves.

But Gretchen didn't feel new and fresh. She felt old and stale. Two more days and the play would be over, thank goodness. That was the way she was thinking of it—as if it were a trip to the dentist.

When the dismissal bell rang that afternoon, Gretchen walked down the stairs and into the gym with Beth. Mrs. McEvoy was already seated at the old upright piano beside the stage. Beth helped Gretchen set up the props for scene 1, and Gretchen helped Beth carry the spotlight on its tall stand to the back of the gym. Kathy and Amy came in and sat down on the edge of the stage. Dennis slouched in, but Miss DiGrassi did not appear.

Then the girl who was playing the mother pushed open

90

the gym door. "Where's Miss DiGrassi?" Beth's voice echoed from the high ceiling.

"She's sick," the other girl called back. "Where's Mrs. Sheppard?"

"She isn't here." Beth turned to Gretchen. "I guess we can't rehearse today."

That was enough for Dennis, who had already started slouching back toward the door. He turned to call, "See you later, losers!"—and almost bumped into Mrs. Sheppard.

"I don't know why no one told *me*—is everyone here for rehearsal?" The teacher hurried across the gym floor toward the stage, waving a copy of the script in one hand and a clipboard in the other. "People, I'm standing in for Miss DiGrassi today, since she's not feeling quite well. I'm sure she'll be fine tomorrow. Now let's make the best use of our time, because the play is the day after tomorrow."

"Thanks for the news flash," whispered Beth to Gretchen.

Mrs. Sheppard looked at a list on her clipboard. "Scenery manager, set up the scenery for scene 1." She looked at Gretchen's feet. "I believe that's Gretchen Nichols."

"The scenery is all set up, Mrs. Sheppard," said Gretchen. What a good thing it was that Miss DiGrassi, not Mrs. Sheppard, was directing the play.

"Oh." Mrs. Sheppard glanced at the stage and pushed her glasses up on her nose. "Let's start at scene 1 and go right through the play. Polly and Winnie Winsum, onstage."

Amy, still sitting on the edge of the stage, got to her feet. Dennis started to trudge up the steps to the stage.

"No, Dennis, did I say your name?" Mrs. Sheppard's voice was sharp and nervous.

Dennis shrugged and trudged down the steps. But a girl from Miss DiGrassi's classroom said primly, "Miss DiGrassi told Dennis to stand in the wings until his entrance cue."

"Oh," said Mrs. Sheppard. "He's in this scene? All right, Dennis." Dennis shrugged again, rolled his eyes and trudged back up the steps to the wings. Beth smothered a giggle.

The whole rehearsal went that way. Each time Mrs. Sheppard gave them a direction, one of the children would say, "But Miss DiGrassi told us—" Then Mrs. Sheppard would press her lips tightly together and push up her glasses with a jab of her finger. At the end of the rehearsal, she said, more loudly than she needed to, "I'm sure Miss DiGrassi will be back for the dress rehearsal tomorrow."

But the next afternoon Miss DiGrassi was still sick. "Mrs. Sheppard, is Miss DiGrassi going to be well enough to come tomorrow?" asked one of the girls from the other teacher's class.

"Of *course* she is." Mrs. Sheppard looked as though she would go to Miss DiGrassi's house and drag her out of bed if necessary. "I talked to her on the phone this morning, and she assured me she would pull herself together for the performance. 'The show must go on!' she said. So of course she'll be here tomorrow. Everyone ready for scene 1?"

"Mrs. Sheppard," said Beth, "I can't find the spotlight!"

"What do you mean?" The teacher whirled to face Beth. "The spotlight must be there. How could it get lost? It's too big to get lost."

"It's not lost, it's gone." Holding a braid with each hand,

Beth looked stubbornly at Mrs. Sheppard. "I always put it backstage by the gymnastics mats, and it isn't there."

"All right, it's gone. We'll have to worry about that later. Everyone in scene 1, onstage."

"But Mrs. Sheppard," said the girl who played Winnie Winsum, "this is the dress rehearsal. Where are the costumes?"

"Where are the costumes?" Mrs. Sheppard looked as if her glasses were going to fall right off her face. "*Where* are the costumes?"

Gretchen sat in the middle of the gym floor, watching Mrs. Sheppard. Maybe it's just as well I'm not in the play, she thought. If Miss DiGrassi doesn't come back, it's going to be terrible. It's going to be the worst play the fifth grade ever put on.

But Amy spoke up. "My mother was supposed to bring the costumes, Mrs. Sheppard. I think she was going to leave them in the office."

Mrs. Sheppard almost ran to the office, the children trailing after her. Sure enough, the costumes were there, in a pile of labeled boxes and bags. With only a little confusion, the teacher handed out the costumes and sent the cast to the rest rooms to change.

Then Mrs. Sheppard looked around at the rest of the children. "Well. You're all understudies, aren't you? Miss DiGrassi's illness made me think we'd better go over your parts, too. This flu is going around. But of course you've been rehearsing right along."

"We haven't been rehearsing at all," said Beth matter-of-factly. "Miss DiGrassi said she didn't have time to rehearse two casts, so we would just have to pick up the lines."

Mrs. Sheppard gasped. "Not at all? Back to the stage, right now! You're going through the play at least once." Shuddering as if she could imagine every one of the main cast sick in bed, she led the understudies back to the gym.

So Beth and Gretchen climbed up on the stage for scene 1. Gretchen's heart began to race. And the minute she said her first line, all her dashed hopes rose up again. She was the perfect Polly Winsum, sweet and good and charming. She heard her own voice carrying so clearly to the back of the gym—to those rows and rows of people who would fill the room tomorrow afternoon.

But Gretchen was the only understudy who knew her part. She had to prompt Beth a few times, and she whispered whole lines to the boy playing the villain. Having missed most of the rehearsals, he was even worse than Dennis.

Gretchen wanted to go on playing Polly Winsum all afternoon, but before the end of scene 1 the cast was back in the gym with their costumes on. "Mrs. Sheppard, shouldn't we start the dress rehearsal?" asked Kathy, swishing her ruffled skirt. "It's getting late."

The teacher looked distracted. "Oh, dear. I suppose we should. But you understudies are terrible!" She paused, pushing her glasses up. "Almost all of you."

Mrs. Sheppard doesn't even like to say my name, thought Gretchen. As she climbed down from the stage, Amy brushed past her, holding up the skirt of her long dress. Amy looks just right for the part, thought Gretchen with a pang. The blonde curls of her wig hung over the ruffled shoulders of her white dress, sprigged with little pink flowers. But I would look like Polly Winsum, too, if I were wearing that dress and that wig. Gretchen ached with envy.

Then an idea shot through Gretchen's mind like an electric shock. She stood staring straight ahead. If something happened to Amy, Gretchen would play the heroine! After all, she was the understudy.

What could happen to Amy? Before Gretchen could stop herself, ideas popped into her mind. Amy could fall off the jungle gym tomorrow at recess and break her arm. Could she get lost in the woods behind the playground if someone led her in deep enough? She could accidentally get shut in the janitor's broom closet.

What crazy ideas. Sighing, Gretchen sank down on the gym floor beside Beth and leaned back against the wall. She couldn't do anything that awful to Amy. Anyway, if she did, Mrs. Sheppard and Mrs. Probola and Mr. Mixell would find out, and they'd probably have Gretchen sent to reform school.

Roars of laughter interrupted Gretchen's thoughts. Looking up, she saw Amy standing in front of the cardboard stove, holding the oven door with a pot holder. The door had come off in her hand.

Even Beth's mother, at the piano, was chuckling, but Mrs. Sheppard didn't laugh. "Scenery manager!" she rapped out. "Aren't you supposed to keep these things in good repair? I expect you to stay after the rehearsal and mend the oven."

Beth gave Gretchen a sympathetic glance, but Gretchen shrugged. That was just the way she expected Mrs. Sheppard to treat her.

Onstage, Dennis was slouching into the Winsum cottage. There were snickers from the other children at the sight of Dennis in a long black cape and top hat. "Swirl your cape

96

around, Dennis!'' called Mrs. Sheppard. "And where's your mustache?''

Scowling, Dennis gave his cape a half-hearted flip. He dug into his pocket and pulled out something that looked like a hairy caterpillar. "It wouldn't stay on."

The teacher sighed, folding her arms. "All right. Just don't lose it. I'll bring some glue tomorrow and stick it on tight. Let's go over that entrance again—and try to put some expression into it.''

Dennis seemed to have forgotten even the lines he knew yesterday. Every time Mrs. Sheppard had to prompt him, her voice was a little sharper.

He's embarrassed about wearing that costume, thought Gretchen. Poor Dennis. Quietly getting up and slipping backstage, Gretchen stood in the wings and began to whisper Dennis's lines to him. Amy and Dennis make quite a pair, she thought. Amy's acting like a windup doll, and Dennis is trying to pretend it isn't really him up on the stage in a sissy costume.

After the rehearsal, Beth helped Gretchen tape the oven door back on. Gretchen thought Mrs. Sheppard had left the gym, but when she looked up, the teacher was leaning on the edge of the stage.

"There you are, Gretchen." The teacher looked embarrassed. "You'll have to prompt Dennis tomorrow afternoon the way you did today. He doesn't know his lines at all. I can't imagine— Of course, Miss DiGrassi will be in charge tomorrow, but I'm sure she would want you to do it, too." Her eyes still did not meet Gretchen's.

Later, as Gretchen trotted past a bed of tulips on Maple Avenue, her thoughts about something happening to Amy slipped back into her head. I wouldn't be able to prompt Dennis if—just supposing—if Amy couldn't be in the play, and I took the part of Polly Winsum. Amy *might* come down with the flu. If Miss DiGrassi can get sick, so can Amy.

For the first time in weeks, a faint hope fluttered in Gretchen's chest.

Slowing to a walk as she passed the Congregational church, Gretchen frowned. White letters on the signboard announced the title of the next sermon: Is Religion Wishful Thinking? That was what she was doing—wishful thinking. Wishful thinking couldn't make Amy get sick.

But magic could.

Gretchen stopped in her tracks. Errora could do it! Errora could give Amy the flu—no, the chicken pox. A little case of chicken pox, like the one Gretchen had in second grade. Gretchen didn't want to make Amy really sick. She just wanted to keep her out of school until after the play.

With a burst of energy, Gretchen shot around the corner, onto Thatcher Lane. That was it, chicken pox! All the time and trouble she and Errora had wasted on cutting hair and changing bodies, when the real solution was so simple. Chicken pox.

Thoughts chattered in Gretchen's head as her sneakers pounded the sidewalk. She had to get to her bedroom and call Errora. Would she come back?

In the house Gretchen waved a hello to her mother on her way to the stairs. "Don't you want a snack?" called Mrs. Nichols. "I actually made cookies."

"Later," Gretchen called back. She closed her bedroom door. "Errora," she said softly, so her mother wouldn't hear. "Errora, please come!"

98

She waited, looking around the room for a hint of a figure in a baggy blue suit. But the air remained empty.

What had she said the first time? She had been looking in the mirror. . . . Gretchen moved in front of the mirror. "Errora, it's me, Gretchen! Help!"

But still there was no answer.

Errora had to come—she had to! If she came, Gretchen would be the star of the play tomorrow. If she didn't, Gretchen would be hauling scenery and whispering Dennis's lines to him. She *had* to hear Gretchen and come! "Errora! Errora! ERRORA!"

The name rang in her ears in the silence that followed. Then there was a sharp knock at the door. "Gretchen, what in the world is all that noise about?"

Mom had heard! Gretchen ran to open the door. "Oh . . . hi, Mom."

Her mother, balancing Jason on one hip, gave her an irritated look. "Why are you roaring like that? You're going to shake the house down."

"I'm sorry." Gretchen flushed. "I—I was just pretending something. See? *Roar!*" She made a fierce lion face at Jason. "I was making wild animal noises."

"All right," said Mrs. Nichols. "Please keep it down to a *dull* roar. I thought you'd hurt yourself."

As soon as the door closed, Gretchen flung herself face-down on the bed. Errora was not going to come.

Or worse—maybe there was no such person as Errora. Maybe Gretchen was a little crazy. No one else had seen Errora. Had those strange things that happened in March really been caused by magic?

Maybe Gretchen had gotten completely confused—

99

maybe it *had* been her attacking Amy and pulling her hair, as everyone else thought.

Then a light like the light from a movie projector fell across Gretchen's pillow. She hardly dared to turn around and look.

"You extended a call for assistance?" Errora's voice was breathless.

II

Solution: Chicken Pox

"Errora?" Sudden hope made Gretchen catch her breath. She rolled over. "Errora, you—" Gretchen stopped, puzzled.

That was Errora, all right, hovering at the foot of Gretchen's bed, clutching her Enchantulator. But she looked different. Instead of the baggy, drab blue uniform, she was wearing a short, pleated skirt and a white blouse. There was no cap on her head, and her hair hung loose around her shoulders. She looked much younger.

In fact, she looked no older than Gretchen.

"Sh!" Placing a finger over her lips, Errora glanced behind her, although there was nothing Gretchen could see except the outline of her desk. "I'm afraid Aunt Injuncta's catching on to me."

Gretchen felt something dawning on her. "What do you mean, 'catching on'? Who *is* Aunt Injuncta, anyway? Why are you wearing different clothes?"

Forcing a smile, Errora waved her hand. "It is my personal feeling that our topic of discussion should focus on a more meaningful area. Tell me about the play."

Gretchen didn't answer at first. She couldn't get over how different Errora looked. Then, as her eyes moved from Errora's plump legs to her plump young face, bits and pieces fell into place in her mind. She felt an angry flush heating her face. "You—you're not a fairy godmother at all, are you? You were just dressed up in someone else's clothes!"

Gulping, Errora backed away from the foot of Gretchen's bed. "Maybe I'm not quite a fairy godmother yet, but I will be, a very important one. My Aunt Injuncta is the Director of the Agency."

"I believe it," said Gretchen. "Because I bet you took her Enchantulator, and I bet you were wearing her uniform. And I bet you're going to be in big trouble when she finds out."

At this, Errora's round cheeks quivered. "I—I'm afraid she suspects. She locked her closet, so I couldn't borrow a uniform. But you wouldn't tell her, would you? Since I've been so helpful, getting you the part you wanted in the play?"

"Wouldn't I?" Gretchen folded her arms. "You didn't help me one bit. Changing with Amy didn't work. I couldn't stand being her. And now everyone thinks I'm a spoiled brat, and I'm still not going to be in the play. I'm much worse off than I was before!"

"Oh, no." Errora's voice was a croak. "The spell went wrong again?" She bit her lip. "This seemed like such a simple case. I did very well in Basic Spells and Approaches

102

to Problem Solving, you know," she added with a touch of pride. "So when your first call came through, and I was practicing on Aunt Injuncta's spare Enchantulator . . . I thought if I did a good job on the case, Aunt Injuncta would be so proud of me, she wouldn't punish me."

Gretchen felt cold tingles run down her spine. So Errora was just as young as she looked. Much too young to be a fairy godmother. Letting Errora work magic on her was like —like flying in an airplane piloted by Dennis Boyd.

"So I ducked back to Aunt Injuncta's chamber," Errora was saying, "and borrowed a uniform—and that's how it happened. I—I just wanted to help you." She looked at Gretchen anxiously.

"No, you didn't," said Gretchen indignantly. "You just wanted to show off. And you didn't know what you were doing. I'd like to tell your Aunt Injuncta exactly what happened."

"Oh, no, please!" Leaning toward Gretchen, Errora clasped her hands pleadingly. "Don't tell her! She'll send me away from the Agency. She'll apprentice me to the Tooth Fairies! Then I'll never become a fairy godmother. Oh, please! I'll do—"

Gretchen stared stonily at Errora.

"I'll do anything," whispered Errora.

Anything. Gretchen had almost forgotten about the chicken pox—the very reason she had called for Errora.

But now Gretchen knew Errora had just been playacting the part of fairy godmother. She felt a twinge of fear. Wouldn't it be dangerous to ask Errora to work any more magic?

Then, in a surge of longing, Gretchen saw herself standing on the stage in Polly Winsum's long, white, ruffled dress, looking out over the rows of parents and children. They were clapping, clapping, clapping—for her.

The play was tomorrow. This was her last chance. Take it or leave it.

"All right," Gretchen told Errora. "You don't deserve it, but all right—I'll help you. I'll tell your aunt I never heard of you and I don't believe in fairy godmothers anyway. That is, I'll help you if you'll help me—if you'll give Amy Sacher the chicken pox."

"Chicken pox?" Errora stared at Gretchen in dismay, slowly shaking her head. "A disease? I—I'm sure that couldn't be the solution."

"It is, though," said Gretchen. "Problem: Understudy can't play Polly Winsum unless Amy gets sick. Solution: Give Amy chicken pox."

"No, no. I'll show you." Errora bent over the Enchantulator, poking keys feverishly. Then a red light flashed from the panel, and the device began to sound a warning *beep—beep—beep.*

"It *is* the solution." Errora spoke in such a low voice that Gretchen could hardly hear her over the beeping. "But I can't do it. I'm not allowed to. That spell is for advanced certified agents only." She shivered.

But Gretchen was thinking only of Polly Winsum. "Okay. Have fun with the Tooth Fairies."

There was a long pause. Errora pushed a button on the Enchantulator, and the warning beep stopped. Then she let out a sigh. "All right . . . I'll try. I need Amy's picture again." She added hopefully, "Maybe you've lost it?"

Smiling, Gretchen jumped up from the bed, pulled her

104

class picture from her bottom desk drawer, and propped it against the pencil holder. "There you go. This is a better one—it's even in color."

Errora gazed at the photograph. "The child with the short blonde hair?" she asked unhappily.

"Yes. You cut it yourself, remember?"

Errora nodded glumly. Her arm trembling, she held the Enchantulator out in front of her. Then a thought seemed to strike her, and her face brightened. "This spell won't take effect until tomorrow morning. Maybe that would be too late."

"Tomorrow morning is fine," said Gretchen. "Don't worry." She ignored Errora's anxious, almost desperate expression.

Clutching the Enchantulator, Errora swallowed. "You'd better get back—way back." She frowned at the picture of Mrs. Sheppard's class. "Amy has short blonde hair. And a plaid shirt?"

"I guess so," said Gretchen, sitting down on the bed. She couldn't see the picture from there. "Yes, now I remember —she was wearing a plaid blouse that day." Something flashed across the edge of Gretchen's mind and then was gone—something to do with the plaid.

Errora jabbed the keys of the Enchantulator. Her face was pale and tight. "Close your eyes! If the light goes haywire—"

Alarmed, Gretchen squeezed her eyes shut. This spell must be a dangerous one. She heard Errora panting and Errora's fingers tapping on the keys. In the darkness in front of her closed eyes, Gretchen imagined Amy's face.

Big brown eyes under blonde bangs. Red spots all over

her cheeks. Red spots. But hard as Gretchen concentrated, the spots danced just to the side of Amy's face, like a cloud of gnats refusing to light.

"There," gasped Errora.

Opening her eyes, Gretchen saw Errora gripping the Enchantulator with both hands. A thin but very bright stream of light shot like a laser beam out of the edge of the Enchantulator toward the picture. In a quavering voice, Errora chanted,

> Initially there exists a condition of discomfort in
>   the area of the head,
> Consequently causing the desire for a period
>   in which rest could be obtained.
> Following this, an increase in body-located
>   temperature
> Shall become evident as a function of direct experience.

"Just a *little* case of chicken pox," said Gretchen uneasily, but Errora didn't seem to hear. Her forehead shone with perspiration, and a lock of hair fell over one eye. Gretchen could see she was hanging on to the Enchantulator as hard as she could, but it bucked and throbbed in her hands like a chain saw. Errora took a deep breath and went on:

> To finalize, differential coloring of a reddish nature
> Is to be seen in an ever-growing extent in the facial
>   context!

There was a crackling flash from the Enchantulator, and a *ping!* like a light bulb exploding. Gretchen and Errora stared in horror at the piece of wreckage in Errora's hand.

The casing of the Enchantulator was shattered, and several keys had popped out from the panel, leaning every which way.

"Oh, no," moaned Errora. "Aunt Injuncta's Enchantulator!" Vainly she tried to press the keys back into the panel. Then she froze, her head on one side. "Did you hear something?"

Gretchen was about to say no when she distinctly heard a woman's voice. It sounded far away and hollow, as if it were coming through a tunnel, but still Gretchen could tell it was angry. Very angry.

"Errora! Pursuant to avoiding negative consequences, it is strongly advised that you return to the Agency!"

Throwing Gretchen a frightened look, Errora vanished. "Remember, you promised." Her voice hung in the air.

Gretchen sat on the edge of the bed, feeling goose bumps run over her arms. Well, it was done. Amy was going to get the chicken pox. And Errora was going to get it from her Aunt Injuncta.

Too bad for them, Gretchen told herself. This was not the time to start feeling sorry for somebody else. *She* was going to play Polly Winsum tomorrow, and it would be the most wonderful moment of her life. She deserved it, after all she had been through.

After dinner that night, Gretchen came up behind her father, who was leaning back in the rocker. She put her arms around his neck. "Daddy, do you think you could take off from work and come to the play tomorrow?"

Tilting his head back, her father gazed at her upside down. "Hm. You look funny with your mouth on your forehead, Gretchen. I thought you wouldn't want me to

107

come to the play, since you weren't going to be in it."

Gretchen smiled smugly. "Well, I do want you to come! I might have a big part after all. If Amy gets sick, I'll play the heroine, because I'm her understudy."

Mr. Nichols' eyebrows went up. "Do you have a voodoo doll up in your room that you're sticking pins in or something?" he asked teasingly.

Gretchen wished he hadn't said that, but she made herself laugh. "You batbrain. Just come to the play, all right?"

12

Errora's Error

The next morning the air was balmy, and billowing clouds drifted across the sky. On the lawn of the Congregational church, the pink dogwoods were in bloom. Taking deep breaths, Gretchen jumped over the lines on the sidewalk. This beautiful morning seemed to be focused on her, the way Beth's spotlight would be focused on her this afternoon.

That is, if Errora's last spell had worked before the Enchantulator broke.

Of course it had worked. Just the same, Gretchen started to run.

Shoving open the front door of the school, Gretchen raced up the stairs to Mrs. Sheppard's classroom. She didn't want to waste a minute. As soon as Mrs. Sheppard discovered Amy was absent, Gretchen could start getting ready to play her part. She yanked open the classroom door—and bumped into someone standing just inside.

"Oof!" The other girl turned around, an indignant look in her brown eyes.

It was Amy.

And her face was creamy smooth. Not even one tiny spot.

But Gretchen couldn't stand here staring at Amy like a dummy. "Sorry," she mumbled. She turned away and dropped into her seat. *What was Amy doing at school, when she was supposed to be home with the chicken pox?* Had the Enchantulator broken before the spell was set, after all?

Take it easy, Gretchen told herself. She managed a smile for Beth, sitting down beside her. Amy must have the chicken pox—she just hadn't broken out yet. The spots would start popping any minute now.

What if they didn't break out until after the play was over this afternoon?

No, they had to break out this morning. Errora had said the spell would take effect this morning. Leaning back in her chair, Gretchen strained her eyes to examine Amy's face again. Kathy caught her looking and whispered something to Amy. Flushing, Gretchen bent over her book bag.

"People." Mrs. Sheppard's voice squeaked. She cleared her throat. "Let's try to settle down and work this morning, although I know we're all excited about the play. I'm sorry" —she cleared her throat again—"*very* sorry to say that Miss DiGrassi is in the hospital with pneumonia, but I think the nicest thing we can do for her is to go on with the show. Yes, Beth?"

"What about the spotlight?" asked Beth.

Gretchen looked at her in amazement. What did the spotlight matter, compared with the bad news that Mrs. Sheppard would be directing the play?

But Mrs. Sheppard looked a little happier. "Oh, yes. That's the good news this morning—the spotlight turned up at the high school, and we have it back." She let out her breath. "Well. Who's the paper monitor today? Please pass out lined paper. Name and date at the top, people."

But the class was only a few words into the spelling quiz when Dennis raised his hand. "Please wait until after the quiz, Dennis," said the teacher in her I'm-trying-to-be-patient tone.

"I don't feel very good, Mrs. Sheppard," he blurted out.

His tone was so pitiful, so unlike Dennis-the-Menace Boyd, that Gretchen stared at him. He didn't look very good. His eyes were glazed, and his face was . . . blotchy.

Walking over to Dennis's table, Mrs. Sheppard peered down at him. "Why, Dennis, you certainly don't look well. You look like—" Then she drew back, suspicion on her face. "Dennis. Tell me the truth. Did you make those spots on your face with a red felt pen?"

There were giggles around the classroom at the idea of Dennis putting red spots on his face to fool the teacher. But Dennis didn't laugh. "No, honest." He rested his forehead in his hands. "My head aches."

The teacher put a hand on the shoulder of his plaid shirt. "I can see you don't feel well, Dennis. You may go down to the nurse." As Dennis pulled himself slowly out of his seat, she looked around the room. "I didn't know chicken pox was going around. Is this the first case?"

Chicken pox!

Gretchen gasped, staring at the back of Dennis's plaid flannel shirt in the doorway. The door swung closed behind him, but the plaid stayed before her eyes. It was—it was the same shirt Dennis had worn the day of the class picture.

Dennis had short blond hair like Amy.

"Amy has short blonde hair. And a plaid shirt?" Errora had asked as she looked at the class picture.

"Oh, no!" moaned Gretchen. Everyone turned to stare at her.

"What is it, Gretchen?" Alarmed, the teacher started toward her. "Don't you feel well either?"

There was, as a matter of fact, a sickening feeling in the pit of Gretchen's stomach. "No . . . I'm sorry." With an effort, she pulled herself together. "I—I was just thinking about the play."

"The *play.*" Now Mrs. Sheppard looked stricken. "Dennis is the villain!" She sat down heavily on the edge of her desk, looking into space over their heads. Finally she said unhappily, "Well, Dennis's understudy will just have to take over." Her gaze fell on Gretchen again. "You're going to prompt him, aren't you, Gretchen? We'll get through—I'm sure the play will go just fine." Drawing herself up, she glanced down at the paper in her hand. "Where were we in the spelling quiz? Word number four? *Neighbor.* Kathy is playing the Winsums' *neighbor.*"

Gretchen stared at her paper until the blue lines seemed to leap out from the yellow background. No! It couldn't be happening this way, just because of a stupid mistake in Errora's spell. If only she had gotten up from the bed and checked what Errora was looking at! If she had done that, Amy would be in the nurse's office right now, waiting for her mother to pick her up and take her home.

"Number five." Mrs. Sheppard's precise voice broke into Gretchen's thoughts. "*Mustache.* Hair on the upper lip is called a *mustache.*"

If only Errora had been more careful. If only a real fairy godmother, instead of that nitwit Errora, had answered Gretchen's call in the first place!

"Cadmun Blackheart has a *mustache,*" said Mrs. Sheppard. "Did everyone get that?"

Miserable, Gretchen wrote the word down. The only good thing was that Dennis would get out of having to wear his silly costume and mustache. He'd be happy about that. At least someone would be happy. Gretchen felt too low even to cry. Her mother and father were coming to the play, too, and she wouldn't be in it.

Later in the morning, Beth's whisper cut through the fog of despair around Gretchen. "Why is Mrs. Sheppard staring at you?"

Mrs. Sheppard, who had spent the last two months *not* looking at Gretchen, now staring at her? But Beth was right. Over and over, as the teacher worked with the reading groups, her eyes wandered toward Gretchen. Mrs. Sheppard looked thoughtful—hopeful, as though she were trying to work something out.

The teacher's gaze made Gretchen uneasy, but she felt a tiny spark of hope. Maybe, in some strange, roundabout way, Errora's magic would finally work to give Gretchen the part of Polly Winsum. What was going through the teacher's mind—was she realizing how much better the play would be if Gretchen were the star?

That's a pretty crazy hope, the sensible part of Gretchen told her. Don't count on it.

But as the children lined up for lunch, Mrs. Sheppard beckoned to Gretchen. "Gretchen, could I speak to you for just a minute, please?" She smiled in a stiff, anxious way.

113

Heart thumping, Gretchen stepped up to the teacher's desk. Why, yes, Mrs. Sheppard, she would answer graciously, I'll be glad to play Polly Winsum.

Behind her pink-lensed glasses, Mrs. Sheppard's eyes looked even redder than usual. "Gretchen, I'm sure you want to cooperate to make this fifth grade play every bit as good as it can be."

Gretchen nodded. Just go ahead and ask me, she said silently.

Mrs. Sheppard's smile relaxed. "I hoped—I knew you wouldn't mind playing Cadmun Blackheart. You know the part so well, and Dennis's understudy is—well, frankly—"

Gretchen stared stupidly at the teacher. Mrs. Sheppard's voice was blocked out by the buzzing in Gretchen's head. Cadmun Blackheart! She, Gretchen, get up on the stage in front of everyone, wearing a top hat and—and a mustache? "No." The word came out of her mouth in a squawk. She backed away from the teacher's desk. "No!"

"But—Gretchen!"

Unwillingly, Gretchen's eyes met Mrs. Sheppard's.

"If—if only you would do it . . . It would make the difference between just muddling through and a performance that Mr. Mixell—that we all can be proud of." With a visible effort, the teacher forced out one more word. "Please."

Mrs. Sheppard was in Gretchen's power. For an instant, Gretchen felt an urge to squash her like a mosquito. Mrs. Sheppard was admitting it: She needed Gretchen to make the play even halfway decent. To play the humiliating part of Cadmun Blackheart.

So let *her* get up on the stage and make a fool of herself!

114

If Mrs. Sheppard was so concerned, let her paste the mustache on her own face!

Then, in spite of the way the teacher had treated her, Gretchen felt a wave of pity for Mrs. Sheppard. It must be awful for her to come into this classroom day after day when she didn't even like fifth graders. She must wish she were back with her sweet little second graders. And it must be awful to be so nervous about what the principal would think.

Well, why shouldn't Gretchen play the villain? Her chance to be the star was gone, anyway. And she could keep the play from being a flop. Gretchen found herself opening her mouth. "All right."

Relief flooded Mrs. Sheppard's face. "Thank you!" Jumping up from her chair, the teacher pressed Gretchen's reluctant hand. "Let's go try the black suit right now—it should fit you pretty well, I think."

Shortly after recess, the children in the play went to the rest rooms to put on their costumes. "Mrs. Sacher will make you up," said Mrs. Sheppard. "Come to the gym as soon as you're ready."

All the other girls carried their old-fashioned ruffled dresses, holding up the long skirts to keep them from dragging on the floor. Gretchen, looking grimly straight ahead, carried the black suit and cape and top hat. Dressing in the rest room, she watched gloomily as Amy's mother went from one girl to the other, applying lipstick and rouge.

Then Mrs. Sacher stopped in front of Gretchen. She must think I'm the perfect one to play the villain, thought Gretchen.

Mrs. Sacher's eyes were cold, but she only said, "Take off

that hat—I'm going to slick your hair down with Vaseline and part it in the middle. . . . Now white powder on your face . . . and dark eyebrows . . . I thought I brought in a mustache with this costume."

Putting her hand in the pocket of the black coat, Gretchen touched something hairy. She shuddered. "I've got it—Mrs. Sheppard's going to glue it on." Maybe the teacher would forget.

Mrs. Sacher picked up the dark brown eye shadow. "Some of this on your cheeks will make your face look thinner. . . . And you need mean lines around your mouth and between your eyebrows. . . ."

The other girls clustered around, watching. When Mrs. Sacher had finished, there was a moment of silence. Gretchen glared around the circle, daring them to laugh, but they only looked amazed.

Then Kathy snickered. But before she could make any smart remarks, Mrs. Sacher said, "Aren't you girls supposed to go to the gym? Scoot along. Sugar—give Mother a kiss for good luck."

For a creepy moment, Gretchen thought Mrs. Sacher was talking to her; but of course she meant Amy.

As the girls hurried through the hall, Gretchen hung back from the others. She could imagine all too well what Kathy was whispering to Amy. Gretchen burned with resentment.

In the gym, Mrs. Sheppard was scurrying back and forth like an ant in front of the rows of folding chairs. "He was supposed to raise it! I specifically made a point of asking him, just yesterday—"

"What is she talking about?" Gretchen asked Beth.

Doing a double take at Gretchen dressed as Cadmun

Blackheart, Beth popped her bubble gum. "Wow. You make a better villain than Dennis did." Then, realizing that was the wrong thing to say, she went on, "It's the basketball net. See? It's still hanging right in front of the curtain."

"Beth!" Mrs. Sheppard's voice was squeaking again. "Run across the hall to the custodian's room and ask him to please bring the ladder *immediately* to the gym. The parents will be arriving— Hurry!"

As Beth sped off, Gretchen looked enviously after her. Beth was still wearing her jeans and T-shirt. She didn't have to get up on the stage looking ridiculous.

"Gretchen! Where is your mustache?"

The teacher had remembered. Gretchen's heart sank, but she pulled it out of the pocket of the black coat.

Putting both hands to her head, Mrs. Sheppard moaned. "The glue! It's in the room—I don't have time to get it now."

The custodian appeared in the gym doorway, whistling and carrying a ladder. Beth held the door open for him. "Beth!" called Mrs. Sheppard. "Run up to the room and get the glue for Gretchen's mustache."

Beth started out the door, but then she turned and trotted back to where Gretchen and Mrs. Sheppard stood in front of the stage. "I bet it would stick on even better with gum, Mrs. Sheppard." She took the wad of bubble gum from her mouth.

Before Gretchen could protest, Beth was spreading her gum over Gretchen's upper lip, and Mrs. Sheppard was pressing the mustache on top of that. "Oh, Beth, how ingenious. Let's go backstage now, people. Everybody backstage!"

"Except the spotlight technician," said Beth.

"Except—yes." The teacher looked distracted. To the custodian she said coldly, "Thank you so much."

Behind the curtains, the scenery hadn't even been set up. Mrs. Sheppard started giving orders to the stagehands in a frantic whisper. The actors milled around in the wings. Just as two stagehands were setting the stove down in its place, the curtains flew open. The stagehands gaped at the parents and younger children taking their places in the rows of seats. "Is the play starting now, Mommie?" piped a little voice.

"Close the curtains!" Mrs. Sheppard's voice was low but furious. The curtains swung shut. The children backstage choked down giggles, and they heard chuckles from the audience.

Gretchen stood stage left, apart from the others, or as far apart as she could be in the cramped space. Maybe she couldn't save the play from flopping, after all. It looked like it was going to be a humiliating joke. And she herself, Gretchen the Villain, would be the biggest joke of all.

Gretchen put her hand to her upper lip. The mustache was on there for good, probably. Bubble gum never came off. Her stomach clenched as she listened to the rustling and murmuring and the squeaking of folding chairs on the other side of the curtain. It sounded like millions of people. Including Mom and Daddy. Why, why had she asked them to come? It would be so embarrassing for them, the parents of that girl in the mustache.

Amy and Kathy and the others were pushing each other and giggling. "Sh!" said Mrs. Sheppard. "The audience can hear you. Everyone ready?" Amy and the girl playing the mother scurried to their places. The teacher stepped in front of the curtain to introduce the play.

The gym became quiet, and then Gretchen heard the audience clapping. All those hands—all those people watching!

Now the piano was rattling out the melodrama mood-setting music. And now the curtains parted, showing Amy bending over to take a papier-mâché pie from the cardboard oven. The oven door did not come off in her hand. The play had begun.

As helpless as if she were in a nightmare, Gretchen watched the scene roll on toward Cadmun Blackheart's first entrance. She couldn't escape. She was going to have to walk onto that stage with a mustache on her face and greasy hair and say, "Aha, my pretty!" to Amy. Amy would probably die laughing. The audience would roar.

Gretchen clenched her fists. No one cared how she felt. Mrs. Sheppard certainly didn't care. She just wanted to look good in front of the parents and Mr. Mixell. Gretchen scowled at Mrs. Sheppard's back as the teacher peered out from the wings.

Turning, Mrs. Sheppard beckoned to her. "This is your cue coming up!" Her voice was urgent. "Wonderful expression, Gretchen! Just keep your face like that."

On the stage, Polly Winsum, alone in her kitchen, was musing out loud. "How fortunate that Mama and I are able to earn a modest income from the tasty pies we bake. Otherwise, we could never pay Mr. Blackheart, the banker, the mortgage installments on our humble but cozy home."

"Now!" breathed Mrs. Sheppard, giving Gretchen a little push. The low chords for the villain's entrance bonged from the piano.

13

Gretchen to the Rescue

Then Gretchen was out on the stage, squinting in the spotlight. "Aha, my pretty," she said. But her words were drowned in a chorus of hisses and boos. Strangely, no one was laughing.

"Say it again!" whispered Mrs. Sheppard from the wings. "Louder! Twirl your mustache!"

Then something inside Gretchen's mind shifted, like a bolt falling into place. She had had it. Five years of waiting to be the star of the fifth grade play, and here she was, the villain. Well, she felt like a villain. Mean and nasty. Black-hearted.

Flinging her cape around her, Gretchen strode over to Amy. She leaned menacingly toward her. "Aha, my pretty. Heh, heh, heh."

Amy shrank away, looking startled. "Why—why, Banker Blackheart."

"I could not help but overhear," sneered Gretchen. "So your income depends entirely upon these little pies, Miss Winsum?" Looking Amy up and down, Gretchen twirled her mustache. A flashbulb from someone's camera lit the stage even brighter for an instant.

"Ss! Boo! Don't talk to him," called someone in the front rows. That was Daddy's voice! Gretchen's heart leaped up. He didn't sound humiliated that his daughter was wearing a mustache. He sounded excited and happy.

Gretchen felt a surge of energy flow through her. As she spoke her lines, she strolled around the cottage, giving a pie a scornful push, turning to the audience to snicker behind her hand. Amy didn't seem to know how to react—she stood frozen beside the stove all through the scene, staring at Gretchen. But that's fine, thought Gretchen, flipping her cape under Amy's nose. She's supposed to be scared.

When Gretchen finally slunk into the wings with a parting "Heh, heh, heh," Mrs. Sheppard met her, eyes wide with hope. "Marvelous, Gretchen!" The teacher gripped her shoulder. "Mr. Mixell will be so proud!"

In the next scene, Amy began to ham it up. She clasped her hands, rolled her eyes, gave dainty little shrieks when Cadmun Blackheart approached her. At last, Amy was *acting*. And it was Gretchen who was getting her to act!

Gretchen felt as if she could do anything now. The play was rolling along with the smoothness and force of an ocean wave. All of them—the mother, the neighbor, the sheriff, the townspeople—were acting better than they ever had in rehearsal. The audience was clapping, cheering, booing in all the right places. It seemed that nothing could go wrong. Even in the third scene, when a scenery tree fell over backstage with a resounding crash, the actors went on with hardly a hitch.

All too soon, the final scene rose to the climax. The sheriff was dragging Gretchen off the stage, shouting, "There's a place behind bars for the likes of you, ex-Banker Blackheart!"

Gretchen was so sorry it was over. "Curses!" She sneered savagely at the audience, lifting handcuffed hands to twirl her mustache one last time. "Curses! Foiled again!" The audience cheered so long that the other actors had to wait a moment before they went on with the play.

Then Amy was speaking the last line. The curtains swept shut. The clapping began on the other side of the curtains and went on and on.

"Line up for your bow!" said Mrs. Sheppard, herding them into order. "Amy and Gretchen in the middle. Go on, now."

The curtains parted again, and the applause swelled. Blinking in Beth's spotlight, Gretchen bowed. She couldn't stop grinning, in spite of the fact that it pulled the bubble gum on her upper lip and hurt.

Then Mrs. Sheppard stepped from the wings to the edge of the stage, holding up her hand for quiet. "Now that the play is over, I want to thank you one and all for being such a supportive, cooperative audience and participating with us in the fun—and I want to let you in on a secret. The star of our play is a talented girl and real trouper who at the very last minute, due to Dennis Boyd's unfortunate illness, took over the part of the villain Cadmun Blackheart—Gretchen Nichols!"

As the audience began to clap again, Mrs. Sheppard took

Gretchen's hand and pulled her forward from the line of actors. "Heh, heh, heh," said Gretchen, flinging her cape over her shoulder. In spite of the spotlight shining in her eyes, she could dimly see Daddy sitting next to Mom in the front row. He stopped clapping long enough to hold up his thumb and finger joined in a circle—*perfect.*

"Bow," whispered Mrs. Sheppard out of the corner of her mouth. So Gretchen took another bow, and the audience hissed and booed and cheered more loudly than before.

Then the curtain closed for the last time, but that wasn't the end of the glory. On the floor of the gym, a mother came up with her little boy, who wanted Gretchen to autograph his program. Then more and more little kids crowded around Gretchen, holding out their programs.

As Gretchen wrote her name over and over, she heard Kathy's voice somewhere behind her. "I guess the reason it was so good was we really knew how to act," Kathy was saying modestly. "You see, we started a drama club, and we practiced acting every day at recess."

Gretchen grinned to herself.

Then Mom and Daddy were beside her, beaming. "Darling, you were wonderful—what an actor!" Mrs. Nichols hugged her. "Wasn't it lucky you got the villain's part, after all?"

Luckier than you think, thought Gretchen. "It sure was."

"Hey, Gretchen, I think you look good in a mustache." Her father squeezed her tight, whispering in her ear, "You *are* a real trouper! I'm proud of you."

"I'm glad you think I look good in a mustache," said Gretchen, giggling wildly, "because it's stuck on with bubble gum. It won't come off."

Mrs. Nichols looked at her, shaking her head and laughing. "Don't worry, we'll work on it with rubbing alcohol. Darling, you were so wonderful. To think I was worried about you. Oh, hello, Mr. Mixell."

The principal smiled approvingly down at Gretchen. "Well done, Gerda! My congratulations to you."

"Gretchen," said Gretchen, wondering if he remembered her from the day Mrs. Sheppard had dragged Amy-in-Gretchen to his office.

He kept on smiling, not seeming to hear. "So you stepped into the breach at the last minute and saved the play. This is the spirit we like to see at the Standish School—going the extra mile. *Miles* Standish? Ha, ha!" With a firm handshake for Gretchen's father, he moved on.

Exchanging glances, Gretchen and her parents burst out laughing. Then Mr. Nichols stretched his wrist to look at his watch. "I've got to get to the bank before it closes. But let's go out to dinner tonight and celebrate, huh? Can you get a sitter for Jason, Linda?"

So Mr. Nichols left, and Mrs. Nichols waited for Gretchen while she went to the girls' rest room to take off her costume. She put the black suit and cape and top hat carefully back into the costume boxes, but she left all the makeup on her face. She couldn't get the mustache off now, anyway; and besides, she wanted to look like the villain for a little while longer.

Just as Gretchen was about to leave, the door swung open. Amy rustled in, holding up the hem of her white dress. "Gretchen!" An eager expression lit up her face. Then she hesitated, as if she felt shy. "Gretchen, you must be the best actor in the school." She paused, pulling off her long-haired wig and shaking her head. "Mrs. Sheppard should have given you a good part to begin with." Amy paused again, looking at Gretchen, as if expecting her to explain something.

But Gretchen just grinned. "Well, I'm glad she didn't, because then she wouldn't have given me a boy's part. And I really liked being the villain." She was surprised to find herself feeling so friendly toward Amy. "You did a great job yourself. I didn't know you could act that well."

"Neither did I," said Amy. They both laughed. Gretchen thought of their two pictures smiling at each other in the photograph folder and wondered if you could become friends with someone by magic.

"Well, my mother's waiting for me." Gretchen pushed open the door. "See you later."

"See you later."

On the way home with her mother, Gretchen felt as if she were in a triumphal parade, riding down Maple Avenue under the arch of new green leaves. The afternoon sun slanted through the leaves into the car. As they passed the Congregational church, Gretchen smiled and waved at a lady coming down the steps, someone she didn't even know. She felt so kindly—she wanted to do something nice for someone else. Maybe she would send Dennis Boyd a get well card.

After picking up Jason at Mrs. Terrence's, they turned into their own driveway. "If you'll run upstairs and get the alcohol from the bathroom," said Mrs. Nichols, "I'll work on your mustache."

"Okay." Gretchen skipped up the stairs, still buoyed by the energy that had swept her through the play. She almost passed her bedroom without noticing the strange light under the door.

Then Gretchen stopped short. Errora, back again? Gretchen hadn't called her. She was doing just fine without any more magic, thank you.

Reluctantly Gretchen turned the doorknob and peeked inside. She drew in her breath sharply.

Two figures hovered in the middle of her room. The larger one was so large that the top of her visored cap almost brushed the ceiling. Her drab blue uniform bulged and strained, instead of bagging and dragging as it had on Errora. Gazing at the row of medals gleaming on the woman's bolsterlike chest, Gretchen knew this must be Errora's Aunt Injuncta.

In one hand, Injuncta carried an Enchantulator. With the other hand, she gripped the arm of the smaller figure, Errora, who now looked very young indeed. She cast Gretchen a pleading look.

"Where is the client Gretchen of Sector 87?" asked Injuncta as Gretchen stepped into the room. Her voice, like a radio with the volume turned up, made the shade of the lamp on Gretchen's night table quiver.

"I—I'm Gretchen."

"Errora!" Injuncta looked down wrathfully. "You have facilitated the growth of hair in the region of her upper lip!"

Errora began to sniffle. "Honest, Aunt Injuncta—"

"She didn't!" To prove it, Gretchen tried to pull the mustache off. "Ow." She dropped her hand, wincing. "It's just part of a costume."

But Injuncta was not listening. "In spite of the fact that my niece"—she gave Errora's arm a fierce shake—"is withholding, confessionwise, it is clear enough that she has brought disgrace upon the Agency by her imposture and bungling. At the present time, I, Injuncta, in my capacity as

127

Director of the Agency and bearer of our proud standard of service for the past five eons, would like to address the need for making personal amends. First of all, a full and humble apology." Injuncta glared at her niece.

Looking in the direction of Gretchen's feet, Errora began to mumble, as if she had memorized what she was saying. "I, Errora, humbly apologize to Gretchen, the human child I have wronged through my selfishness, irresponsibility, and utter disregard of the rules and regulations of the Agency. I fully admit that I am not fit to take my place in the proud ranks of the Agency, and hereby forfeit my hereditary rights thereto." Errora gulped back a sob.

"The culprit is required to continue," said Injuncta. She looked as relentless as a rhinoceros.

But before Errora could go on, Gretchen burst out, "Excuse me, Mrs. Injuncta. I don't mean to interrupt, but you're making a mistake about Errora. She didn't wrong me at all. She helped me. I'm so glad you brought her here, because I wanted to thank her. Really."

Injuncta's mouth fell open. She looked from Gretchen to Errora and back again. "How can that be? She could not possibly have assessed your situational obstacles correctly— she will not be studying Situational Assessment at the Agency for another two years. Kindly do not attempt to excuse her inexcusable acts."

Gretchen saw that Errora had lifted her head and was staring at her with a spark of hope in her eye. How could she convince Injuncta? "I don't know how Errora did it, but she did it absolutely right. You see, I wanted to be the heroine in the fifth grade play. I tried to get Errora to work a spell so I could play that part—I didn't even care what

129

happened to anyone else. But Errora knew that wouldn't be right, so she worked the spell so I had to play the villain instead. And I didn't want to, but when the play started, I found out how much fun the villain's part was—and the play was a big hit. And Mrs. Sheppard was happy, and Amy was happy, and everyone else was happy, even Dennis, because he didn't want to be in the play. So it worked out for everyone, not just me. So, wasn't that smart of Errora, even if she did borrow your Enchantulator without asking?''

"Errora." Dropping her niece's arm, Injuncta gazed down at her with astonishment. "Why wasn't this input provided prior to the present moment?"

Errora rubbed her arm, looking bewildered. Gretchen hoped she would be able to think of something. Then Errora smiled sadly at her aunt, her face round and innocent. "I tried to, Aunt Injuncta, but you ordered me to behave in a silence-oriented manner."

"Mm," said Injuncta skeptically. "And you always do just as you're told? But never mind. The girl Gretchen's testimony throws quite a different light on your infractions. Breaking the rules of the Agency cannot be treated lightly —still, the fact that so much good was done—" She gazed upward in thought, propping her heavy chin on the edge of the Enchantulator. "I suppose I need not report this case to the Advisory Council, after all. Disciplinary steps will be taken in an atmosphere conducive to privacy." She frowned at Errora.

"But you won't send her away to the Tooth Fairies, will you?" asked Gretchen. "Because she wants more than anything to be a fairy godmother—a really super one like you," she added craftily. "That's how she landed in all this trouble —she couldn't wait to get started."

130

"We must cultivate patience, mustn't we, Niece Errora." Injuncta's tone was sarcastic, but Gretchen thought she saw a smile tugging at the Director's lips. "Very well. Still, Client Gretchen, it is my feeling that the Agency should make amends vis-à-vis the strain you have been under. I, Director Injuncta, will personally assess your situation and address your needs." She smiled at Gretchen, fingering the keys on her Enchantulator.

Although Injuncta's expression was kindly, Gretchen shrank back. "No!" She edged toward the door. "I mean, thank you very much, but I really don't need any more magic. Everything's fine. But thank you very much."

"No?" Injuncta looked astounded. Then she shrugged. "In that case . . . it is almost closing time. Come, Errora." She grasped Errora's hand, much more gently than before.

Errora lifted her free hand to her lips and blew Gretchen a kiss. "In closing, Client Gretchen, please be aware that appreciation exists." She winked.

"You're welcome," said Gretchen, grinning. She blinked—and Errora and Injuncta had vanished.

Then she heard a door slam downstairs. "Where's the meanest villain in town?" called her father. "I want an exclusive interview."

Joy rose in Gretchen's chest. Twirling her mustache, she ran downstairs.

People Called Me A Nut

"My book is not the kind that tells 'How Tomboy Mindy discovered that growing up gracefully can be as fun as playing baseball.'

"I have often thought how relaxing it would be to be invisible. But when I took over Richard's paper route they said 'girls can't deliver papers.' And when I wanted to take tennis instead of slimnastics, they said 'girls like to do graceful feminine things.' So I had to speak out. I only wanted things to be fair.

"My book is for anyone who might want to read about the life and thoughts of a person like me. If some boy wants to read this, go ahead. Maybe you will learn something."

The Real Me
by Betty Miles

An AVON CAMELOT BOOK
Code: 65292-7 • $2.25

"Some kids in our class act as though they can't wait to be teenagers. Some girls even wear green eye shadow to school and pierce their ears. I never want to grow up if that's how you're supposed to act."

The Trouble With Thirteen

by Betty Miles

Annie and her best friend Rachel wish they could stay twelve forever. Everything is perfect ... until unexpected changes begin pulling them apart just when they need each other the most. But through it all, Annie and Rachel learn about independence and loyalty—and some good things about turning thirteen.

An Avon Camelot Book 64626-9 • $2.25

Also by Betty Miles:

Just The Beginning 65276-5 • $2.25
Looking On 65284-6 • $2.25
The Real Me 65292-7 • $2.25
Maudie and Me and The Dirty Book 64071-6 • $2.25

I WOULD IF I COULD

by Betty Miles

When 10-year-old Patty Rader goes to visit her grand-mother in Ohio, she thinks it will be the best summer ever. But, then she doesn't get the big fat-wheeled shiny bike she was expecting. And, to make matters worse, she thinks the stuck-up Staley twins are trying to steal away her best-friend Mary Alice. Now Patty's afraid that this is the *worst* summer ever, until she learns that sometimes what you want is not the most important thing to wish for.

Avon Camelot   **63438-4/$2.25**

Other Avon Camelot books by Betty Miles:
MAUDIE AND ME AND THE DIRTY BOOK 64071-6/$2.25
THE REAL ME   65292-7/$2.25
THE TROUBLE WITH THIRTEEN   64626-9/$2.25